https://kdclark.blog/

King Of The Bronx
by K.D Clark

Sign up for my newsletter to stay up to date on all new releases.

ALSO BY K.D CLARK

Merciless Queen

Twisted Judgement

Apprehension

Savage Spades

Dirty Empire

King of The Bronx

Escaping the Bratva

Hating the Bratva

Loving the Bratva

Penthouse Heist

Chapter One

<u>Raven</u>

I knew something was wrong the moment I put my key into the lock of the front door. It was dead silent on the other side. Usually at least a couple of the girls were awake by now, getting ready for the long night ahead. The door creaked as I opened it. As I took a step inside, glass crunched under my boots. I followed the trail of glass to a broken vase a couple feet in front of me. The front desk was in complete havoc. Papers were flung everywhere, and the few decorations I had were now laying on the floor in pieces. The couch, where men waited for their turn, was flipped upside down. The pillows were thrown astray. I shut the door behind me and continued into the room. All the girls' rooms were upstairs except for Natalie's room, which was to the left of the welcome desk. I turned to run up the flight of stairs to check on the girls when he came around the corner.

"I was wondering when you'd show up." His voice sent chills down my spine. I snapped my eyes shut, hoping this was all a bad nightmare and he would disappear. "Turn around, beautiful. I want to see that face."

My stomach turned, but I did as he asked. The Irish solider stood a few inches taller than me. His arms were covered in thick black hair, and his gut protruded over his belt buckle. He looked like our average client. He ran a hand over his greasy beard.

"You're late on your payment," he said, taking a step closer to me. I took a step back and he paused.

"Don't be scared, Princess, I—"

"Where are my girls?" I snapped, cutting him off. There wasn't any noise coming from upstairs, and that's what scared me the most. I'd vowed to keep the girls at the house safe and so far, I was doing a shitty job at it.

"The girls are fine. I took one for myself, but the rest are upstairs being good little whores."

I squeezed my eyes shut again, willing the tears away. I didn't want to guess which girl he had taken for himself. Just because they worked in a brothel, everyone treated them like they weren't human.

When I opened my eyes again, I jumped at how close he stood next to me. I squared my shoulders, trying to appear strong. This man wanted me to be scared of him, but I couldn't give him that satisfaction. He reached his hand out, almost like he wanted to tuck a loose strain of hair behind my ear. I quickly slapped his hand away. His yellowing teeth showed as he smiled.

"I like when they fight back. Gives me more of a challenge."

"I'll have the money next week," I said. Anything to get this fucker out of the house. I needed to check on my girls. The silence from the floor above us was louder than the man's voice.

"You said that last week and guess what? No money."

He was right. The brothel wasn't exactly doing as well as I thought it would. Not when I refused to cut the girls' pay. They were the ones doing all the hard work. I wasn't going to be like other owners in the area and degrade the women. I'd been in the same situation before once in my life.

"I will have it this time," I gritted out between clenched teeth.

"You know there is another way to pay," he said, taking a step closer. He smelled like garlic and grease. "You could earn at least half of the payment."

My stomach turned, and I thought I was going to be sick. I tried to step back but hit the bottom of the stairs.

"Tell Niall to give me another week. I'll bring the money personally to him," I said, even though the thought of walking into the Irish bar terrified me. I had to keep the Irish away from my brothel. I hated when they showed up like this. If I'd known when I took over the brothel that the Irish were involved, I would have never considered it. I wish I could go back in time and fix my stupid mistake.

"You know, if you'd just let us sell some of your whores, it would cut down your loan by—"

"No," I snapped. It was sick to think about the things men like this did to women. Human trafficking was one of their main sources of income. I wanted nothing to do with it. They'd offered me a position multiple times to oversee the sex trade, but that was too repulsive and low. Even for me.

"Looks like you have bit of a soft spot for your whores, don't you?" He was teasing me like a lion playing with his food before eating it.

"Looks like you have a soft spot for women who'd rather choke on their own vomit than sleep with you."

His teasing smile dropped, and his eyes turned dark. His hand smacked against my face so fast, I barely had time to register the pain. My legs gave out, and my back hit the bottom step on the way down.

"One month. Niall is feeling particularly generous. If I come back, we will take all your whores and sell them across the ocean, including you, to men who make me look like a saint."

The tears threatened to spill from my eyes, but I kept it together, not wanting this man to see me weak. Men like him didn't deserve my tears. He kicked a piece of glass before turning around and walking toward the door.

"You should probably get this place cleaned up too. It's not a good look."

He left out the door, and as soon as it shut, I allowed the tears to roll down my cheek. I'd give myself five minutes—that's all—and then I needed to handle business. I hiccupped as I cried, all the emotion coming out like a tsunami that had been held back by a dam. My cheek burned from his slap, and I knew there was probably a bright red mark across my face. I hated the Irish more than anything else. They were terrible people who got off on threatening the small Irish community. I wiped my face after a moment and stood. I readjusted my T-shirt and ripped jeans, hoping to regain my composure before facing the girls. The women in my brothel had gone through enough in their life, and guilt swirled in my stomach at the thought of putting them through more trauma.

I climbed the wooden steps to the top floor. It was hotter up here than the rest of the building. Ten bedrooms were upstairs, and none of them had doors, just a sheet that hung over the doorway. If a man got too handsy, I wanted to make sure the other girls could hear it. This also made sure he wouldn't try to lock the door.

"He's gone," I said to the empty hallway. The women came out of their rooms and instantly gravitated to me.

Erica got to me first and engulfed me in a big hug. The smell of sweet lavender filled my nose. It was Erica's favorite scent. She said it kept her relaxed.

"Are you okay? I'm so sorry, Raven." Erica wore a silk nightgown with a robe over the top, despite the fact that it was three o'clock in the afternoon. They were all probably still asleep when he'd busted in the front door and started destroying things.

"It's okay. He's gone. We're okay."

"He's going to come back," Erica said.

I swallowed the lump in my throat. I couldn't let him come back, not again. I had to have the money this time. I just had no idea how I was going to get it. I looked around at the girls. I counted nine. They were all women of different shapes and sizes, most coming from the same terrible background I'd come from, and many from foster care or abusive relationships with nowhere else to go. At least here, they had a roof over their heads and money to earn so they could buy the things they needed.

"Where's Evelyn?" I asked.

"In the bathroom...he came up here earlier," Erica said.

I walked past the girls to the shared bathroom at the end of the hall. I knocked on the wooden door, aware of the eyes on my back.

"Evelyn?" I asked. The door opened, and Evelyn stood there with a towel wrapped around her body. Her blond hair was wet and stuck close to her face. She was the smallest of the girls. She'd lost a lot of weight after getting into some bad drugs a while back, but I had a strict rule: No drugs or I'd kick you out. Evelyn had sobered up quickly but hadn't gain any of her weight back. My eyes instantly zoned in on the red mark around her neck.

"Are you okay?"

Evelyn nodded. "Yeah, he has a little dick."

I smiled and pulled her in for a hug. "I'm sorry—"

"It's fine, Raven. It could have been worse—we're fine. The house is still standing. It's okay."

*****

It took two hours to clean up the mess in the lobby area. I bet it only took a matter of minutes for him to completely destroy it. I sat at the front desk, going through paperwork. I had eaten with the girls in the kitchen after they cleaned up, but I needed to focus on the money. All I had was a month to get the Irish the money I owed them. $30,000 dollars. I was surprised that Niall even let the payments get so high. I knew it was because he was just holding out. If he tried to sell my girls, they would bring in four times that amount. I flipped through pages of financial statements and credit card receipts, but there was nothing there. No hidden money or payment anyone owed the brothel. The girls kept seventy-five percent of what the clients paid. The other twenty-five percent went into the business. I took enough home to pay for my apartment and the things I needed on a daily basis, but never more than that. Compared to the foster homes I lived in as a child, this was luxury.

"Are you okay?" Erica asked as she walked toward the desk and leaned against the front.

"Just trying to figure out where to get this money from," I said, leaning back in the chair and putting my hands on top of my head. I needed to think. There was only one person I knew who might loan me the money, and even that was a stretch. The door chimed as a man walked into the house. Erica stood up straight and pushed her chest out. She was naturally pretty with silky black hair and a lean body. Small freckles covered the bridge of her nose and her cheeks. It gave her that young and innocent look. It hadn't taken much for her to get a few regulars.

"How can I help you?" Erica asked her voice low and sultry. The man smiled at her. He was dressed in a business suit. I wondered if he was stopping by before going home to his wife. The man took out a wad of bills and set it on the desk. They always paid first before going upstairs with the girls. I grabbed the money off the desk and counted it before nodding at Erica. She grabbed the man by the hand and led him up the stair, swishing her hips as she did. I counted the money again, set aside twenty-five percent aside, and then rubber-banded the rest together. I wrote Erica's name on the first dollar and set it in the safe under the desk. At the end of the night, I'd give each girl their money. They trusted me to be honest and fair, and I wasn't going to betray that trust no matter how much trouble I was in. If I was in a different part of the country, I probably could have saved up the money to pay the Irish by now. But the rent in New York was so high, I didn't have much leftover for myself.

The night went on, and more men came into the brothel. Usually, one of the girls was downstairs, and they could lead the men to their bedroom just as Erica had. At one point, a couple men waited on the sofa across from my desk for their turn. I had become desensitized to the reality of what was going on at the brothel. Some people might call the women whores, but wasn't it really the men that were the gross ones? They paid to have sex with someone, not even caring about the potential to catch STIs. Men were pigs. The men that came in with nice clothes and watches, I could only assume that they had wives and kids at home. I imagined their wife finishing up dinner while her husband finished up in one of my girls. That's the part of the job that grossed me out, not what went on upstairs. I kept track of the women each time they came down to grab a new client. If one of the girls was up there too long with a man, I'd go check on her.

At 5 a.m., we shut down for the night. The house was open seven days a week from 4 p.m. to five a.m. We don't take holidays off, and Christmas was usually when we were the busiest. Men got lonely during Christmastime when they didn't have any family. I locked the door, said good night to the girls, and walked home. I chose to keep my apartment close to the brothel so that I didn't have to take the subway and I could pop over if there were any issues. I crossed my arms over my chest as the wind blew, lifting up my hair. The sun was just starting to rise, and the streets were almost quiet. The smell of food lingered in the air, and my stomach rumbled. I turned the corner in the opposite direction of the apartment and walked into the empty diner. The bell rang as I opened the door.

"Hey, Raven," the skinny boy at the counter said as he closed the cash drawer.

"Hey, Jeff. You're here early." I took a seat at the counter.

He shrugged. "I got suspended from school, so not much else to do."

I reached over the counter and grabbed his chin. I turned his head so I could see the bruise on his cheek. It was an ugly mix of green and purple. "Fighting again?"

The boy smirked. "Gotta hold my own out there."

New York public schools were notorious for being rough. I knew because I'd gone to public school too. It was either fight or get chewed up and spit out. Most parents sent their kids to private schools, but that could get expensive.

I shook my head. "Where's your dad?"

Jeff pushed his shaggy, brown hair out of his eyes. "Ran to the store real fast. You hungry?"

"Starving."

Jeff turned away from me to grab some ingredients out of the fridge in the back room. He carried all the items to the front and got to work. He didn't need to ask what I wanted.

"Busy night?" he asked after a moment.

"Jeff..." I warned him.

"What? I'm just asking. Usually, customers like to talk about the rough day they had at work."

I rolled my eyes. Despite my best efforts, Jeff knew what I did for work. I've been coming to the diner long enough that things slipped out, and the curious kid put the pieces together. I just hoped he wasn't going around and telling his friends at school. "How about you worry about getting yourself back in school?"

He threw a patty on the grill before washing his hands, then turned to look at me. "I still have a year left. I'll figure it out. So about the girls—"

"That's enough, Jeff."

He shook his head with a smile on his face and went back to making my food.

After I finished my burger and fries, I walked to the apartment. The streets were now full of people rushing to get to work. The cafés were packed with people eager to get their morning coffee. It was my favorite part of the day because I could go inside and sleep while the rest of the world spent their day in a cubicle.

Chapter Two

"Raven! I've missed you." Toby came around the bar to engulf me in a hug. I inhaled his scent of cologne and whiskey. He was the closest thing to a brother I'd ever had. We'd stayed in the same foster home for three years, the longest time I'd been in one place. We stayed in touch, like real siblings. He was much taller than me, and we had completely opposite features. While I was short with long red hair and bright blue eyes, Toby stood well over six feet with short blonde hair and green eyes. He was skinny as a kid, but once he became an adult, he hit the gym on a regular basis. He'd filled out admirably, becoming muscular in all the right places. I doubted he had any trouble getting women at bars. Toby went down a much easier road to business ownership than I had. I pulled back from the hug and tousled his short hair. He swatted my arm away.

"Stop trying to embarrass me," he complained.

I laughed. "That's part of the fun."

The bar was mostly empty because it was still early. Only a couple men sat at the end of the counter, and it looked like they'd been there most of the day.

"Let's get a booth. You want a drink?" he asked.

I shook my head. "No, thanks. I gotta work tonight."

He smiled and led me over to a red booth in the corner. The one thing I loved about Toby was that he never judged me. He knew the business I ran, and although he had taken a different route in life, he never made comments about me.

"So what's up?"

I took a deep breath trying to find my nerve. "I need to ask for a loan," I blurt out as fast as possible. It was like ripping off a Band-Aid. I wanted to get this over with quick.

Toby's smile fell into a deep frown. "The Irish bothering you again?"

I nodded.

He ran a hand over his face. "Shit. How much?"

I picked at the loose nail polish on my fingernail. "$30,000."

His eyes widened, and he ran a hand across his jaw. "How the fuck do you owe them $30,000?"

"I don't know, Toby. I don't even know how much the balance is on the loan."

I'd bought the brothel from an old friend for $10,000. I'd saved up for years to be able to buy it. What my friend didn't mention was that he was deeply in debt with the Irish mob because of it. My "friend" was smart though and skipped town before I could kill him myself.

"What are they going to do if you don't pay?"

"Sell my girls," I admitted.

He closed his eyes as if the thought pained him. "I don't have it. If I did, you know I'd give it to you in a heartbeat so you can get these guys off your back. The bar does okay but not well enough for me to have $30,000 lying around."

I dropped my head and stared down at the wooden tabletop.

"I understand. It's a lot to ask..."

Toby leaned closer to me and lowered his voice to a whisper. "I do have a guy who needs some product moved."

I was shaking my head before he even finished. "I can't run drugs anymore. It's too risky."

"I agree, but it's also risky staying in debt with the Irish."

He was right, but I also didn't want to spend the rest of my life in prison. Moving drugs was something stupid I used to do to make quick cash. Most of the money I managed to save up to buy the brothel was made from getting drugs from one place to another. Toby sat back in the booth as we both stared at each other, but I was lost in my own thoughts. I had no idea how I was supposed to pull this off. The sound of a glass breaking made me jump. I turned my head to see the bartender bend down to clean it up. When I turned back around to face, Toby he was chewing on the side of his mouth.

"What?" I asked.

"What about cards?"

I scoffed. "I'm beyond rusty. It's been years since I've counted."

"So practice, get better, and then get away with the money." He placed his elbows on the table and stared at me.

"I can't—"

"Do you have a better idea?"

I looked down at the table. "No...where would I practice at?"

"I know a place. It's underground."

"That sounds just as risky as smuggling."

"But you're good at it. You won't get caught. Become a regular and lose a bunch in the beginning until you can get your skills up. Then one night, take it all home."

Toby had a point. It was a fast way to get the cash I needed. Back in the day, I used to be the best at counting cards. It took a lot of studying and practice in the beginning, but I'd gotten good at it. It was an easier way of making money than selling myself, which was what a lot of the foster kids ended up doing.

"You really think I can pull it off?" I asked.

"No doubt."

I didn't have many options at this point. Card counting may be my best bet. I had a month to hone my skills and really get good at it again, but the risks were high. If I got caught, it could mean death, especially at an underground place like the type Toby was talking about.

"I'll think about it."

He nodded. "Let me know if you need help with anything. Sorry I can't offer you more."

I stood up from the booth just as he did and gave him a quick hug.

"Oh hey, we're doing a big barbecue here next month if you want to stop by. Bring the girls. We're expecting to be really busy."

"Okay, we'll stop by. See ya ,Toby." I walked out of the bar.

*****

"What are you thinking about?" Erica asked, making me jump. I'd been so focused on my thoughts, I hadn't even noticed Erica walk up to the desk.

"Just thinking." It had been two days since Toby suggested I count cards. He texted me the address, but I was still debating if this was a risk I really wanted to take.

"About the Irish?" Erica asked.

I nodded. "Just a lot on my mind right now."

"We could always give you a bigger cut," Erica suggested.

I shook my head. "No, you ladies are the ones up there doing the work. I'm not a pimp who is going to take all your money. That's dirty."

Erica came around the desk and sat in the chair next to me. "You're a good person, Raven. You'll figure it out."

I had to or else all my girls were going to get sold off, and I couldn't let that happen. I stood up from the desk chair and grabbed my jacket off the back.

"Can you take care of this for a few hours?" I asked. It was a slow night at the house anyways.

Erica nodded. "Yeah, I'll take care of it. Where you going?"

"To make some money."

Chapter Three

<u>Enzo</u>

It took my eyes a moment to adjust to the darkness of the underground gambling room. The few overhead lights were dim. I'd done that on purpose so that the politicians and "upstanding citizens" could better keep hidden. I was used to the celebrities and politicians that came through, gambling away taxpayers' money because it was now an addiction. I couldn't judge; I didn't even pay taxes.

Once my eyes adjusted, I could see every table was filled, which meant a good night for me. I crossed the room, slapping the hands of some of the regulars. I made it to the bar and ordered a water. I choose to stay away from alcohol. I didn't have anything against it. Alcohol just made me sleepy, and I still had work to do before I could call it a night. I thanked the bartender as Tommy took a seat beside me.

"What's good?" I asked Tommy, reaching my hand out for him to slap.

"Nothing much, trying to see if someone shows up."

That caught my interest. "Someone owe you money or something?"

It might turn out to be an exciting night after all.

Tommy shook his head. "Nah, nothing like that."

He didn't elaborate and I didn't push. It was probably business with his crew. Tommy was notorious for avoiding problems. He probably didn't want any extra people involved in whatever it was. He signaled for the bartender, and I turned around to face the room. The gambling ring was underneath a row of shops on the strip. Essentially, it was the connecting basement of the stores. It was a big enough space for six tables. There were only a couple spots open at the blackjack table. Harris was going to have to start turning people away at the door soon.

"Gio tell you about the new Irish boss?" Tommy asked.

"Nah, what's up?" This must be fairly recent if I hadn't heard yet. I knew everything about what happened in this city.

"Gio got a new boss in place. Niall's own son, he took out his dad. Apparently, the guy helped us out. A win-win kind of situation."

Well, fuck, that was convenient. "Because of that chick?" I asked. Everyone had been a little hush-hush about Giovanni's new girlfriend. I just wanted confirmation.

Tommy chuckled. "Fuck yeah. He almost blew my head off because I was talking to her at Lucas's restaurant one day."

"She hot?"

He took a sip of his drink. "I can't answer that. I like all my limbs attached to my body."

I smiled. Well, damn. Giovanni finally settled down.

"I did catch her with Wes, but you didn't hear that from me."

I almost choked on my water. "You got to be shitting me. Wes is a dead man if he was sticking his dick in the boss's girl."

"She said they all had an understanding."

"That's some freaky shit."

My head turned toward the door as it closed. Not much surprised me these day, but a woman walking into my gambling ring made me freeze. Long red hair fell to her waist. She wore heels that made her look tall, but without them, she probably barely reached my chest. The dress she wore showed off every single curve of her body. She walked with her shoulders back, confident, despite the fact that she was the only female in the room. When I looked back out to the floor, I realized she hadn't just caught my attention, but also the attention of every other man in the room.

"Damn," Tommy mumbled next to me. Her heels clicked against the cement floor as she walked to the blackjack table and took a seat. She acted as if she'd been here before, but I was one-hundred-percent certain I'd remember if she'd walked in here before. The men in the room went back to focusing on their cards, but I couldn't tear my eyes away.

"You're drooling," Tommy said.

"Shut the fuck up." I turned away from the woman and grabbed my water to take a drink.

"You know her?" Tommy pushed.

I shook my head. "No, but I'm going to get to know her."

The door shut again. It must have been who Tommy was looking for because he pushed away from the bar and went to greet the man. They both walked back outside together.

I turned and watched the woman, fascinated with her. That long hair would be too easy to pull on. Her hair was so bright, I doubted it was natural. I spend enough time around women to know fake from real. What reason did this woman have to be so confident in a room filled with men with severe gambling problems? My attraction to her mixed with a hint of suspicion. She'd chosen to sit at the open blackjack table. She must know something about cards if she took that seat. I watched from my place at the bar as she pulled out a wad of cash from her purse, counted out the amount she needed to buy in, and slid it to Larry, one of my dealers. They didn't use chips or coins to play here. Cash only, although we did occasional take money in the form of houses or cars. That's how I knew someone's gambling issue had gotten out of hand. When a man would bet the house his family was living in, it was time for him to get treatment. Larry dealt the cards out. It was obvious this wasn't the woman's first time. She peeked at the cards quickly, already memorizing them. They went around the table, each person telling Larry to give them another card or skip them. Afterwards, they flipped the cards over to reveal their hand. The women lost, but she didn't show signs of disappointment or surprise. She accepted it as if it was just part of the game. She either didn't have a gambling problem or had a lot of money to bet. One of the men got up to leave, and I crossed the room to take his spot, right next to Red.

"You in, Boss?" Larry asked.

I nodded, and he went on dealing everyone a new hand of cards. He didn't need to ask for my money. We'd have a problem if he did.

Up close, the woman was even more beautiful. While she was seated, the dress she wore lifted slightly, revealing her creamy legs, which led up to a flat stomach. Her breasts weren't huge, but they were perfect for her body shape. Her thick ruby red lips matched the color of her dress. Her face was perfectly heart-shaped, which gave her a youthful look.

"Can I help you?" she snapped, having caught me staring. Everyone at the table froze, but she didn't seem to realize or care about the mistake she made. I ran the underground, so no one was allowed to talk to me like that.

I smiled at her. "Just admiring your beauty," I said, throwing her one of my typical lines. It wasn't hard for me to win over women. Once they got a look at me and realized who I was, it wasn't long before I took them home.

Her lips twisted into a snare, and she turned away from me to look at her cards. Well, damn. I looked over my cards, bored with the game already. Gambling wasn't my thing. I preferred to make money, not lose it. Larry dealt to those who wanted another card. Red and I both lost the first hand.

"What's a pretty woman like you doing in a place like this?" I asked her. She didn't even bother to turn my way as I spoke.

"Just trying to play the game."

"Most women stay far away from this place. Most don't even know about it." I was digging. She might be beautiful, but this wasn't a spot you just stumbled upon. I had this place well-hidden for a good reason.

She whipped around to look at me. "Is there something you are trying to ask me?" Her voice sliced through the air like a whip. I could feel the tension coming off the men around us, like they were holding their breath. Her sharp attitude only excited me. I liked that I was getting her riled up. Her skin was turning a soft red color that matched the rest of her. A couple men got up from the table, probably uncomfortable with the conversation.

"Maybe we should start over," I suggested.

"Maybe we shouldn't, and you should just let me play my hand."

It took everything in me not to smile. I rested an elbow on the table and leaned my head on my hand. I'd forgotten about Larry and the rest of the men sitting around the table. "I would, but I own this place, Red, and if I ask someone why they're here...I want an answer."

She swallowed as a lump formed in her throat, and I smiled. She should be afraid of me. The Bronx's underground was a dangerous place I'd created years ago. I was the most dangerous part of it all. She looked away, breaking eye contact. I sensed there was something she was afraid to tell me.

Did she have a gambling problem? She didn't look like the typical addict. I reached a hand out and grabbed her chin in between two fingers. She jumped. I steered her head around to look at me. Her blue eyes were glossy with unshed tears. My eyebrows drew together as I tried to figure out what was going on. What had made this woman so desperate to put herself in danger to come here?

I opened my mouth to ask when Harris appeared by my side.

"We got a problem, Boss."

I stared at the women for a moment longer before letting go of her chin and leaving the seat. I walked with Harris until we were out of ear shot.

"What's up?"

"Charles and Leon are getting into it again next door," Harris said.

"Fuck."

I walked out the door and up the stairs to the street above. I owned the bar that was right next door. Harris stayed outside. As soon as I walked in, the sound of loud music filled my ears, but instead of everyone drinking and having a good time, they were staring at the two idiots having a stand-off. Charles had lost his shirt while Leon barely looked capable of standing.

Charles saw me first and his eyes widened. He shifted his position so he wasn't in a fighting stance anymore.

"Don't back down now, pussy," Leon spat.

I walked up to Leon and put a hand on his shoulder. I wasn't much bigger than Leon in size, but that didn't matter when I was the boss. Respect was the most important element of Cosa Nostra. Without it, there would be chaos.

"Both of you, outside. Now," I said as calmly as I could. The people at the bar were just regular people. Unlike the underground, they didn't expect violence. They were just out for a good time.

Leon straightened as if a metal rod had been placed down his spine. I walked out the door and around to the side of the building. Charles rounded the corner first, and I landed a punch to his face. A satisfying crunch filled the air, and blood gushed from his nose.

"Fuck!" he moaned holding the front of his face. Leon was next. As soon as he rounded the corner, I gave him the same treatment.

"What the fuck are you two thinking?" I yelled.

Neither of them answered.

"You can't even go to the same fucking bar without causing a scene."

"Boss, I—"

"Shut the fuck up," I said. "You're both a part of this crew, so stop embarrassing me. If I have to break up a fight again, I'm going to take it as a personal attack against me. Go home and sober up. I'll meet with you both tomorrow at Bella Vita."

"Yes, Boss," they both said as they walked their separate ways. Charles left a trail of blood behind him from his still dripping nose.

I ran a hand over my face. Running a crew of criminals could be the most exhilarating part of my day or the most exhausting. I walked back to the underground, Harris following behind me, but when I got back down there, the woman had disappeared.

*****

I woke to the soft clicking noise of Bello's paws as he paced outside the door. The dog had gotten in a bad habit of sleeping with me a couple months ago, so now, I had to close my bedroom door and hear him pace outside. Nothing ruined a one-night stand as much as a dog crawling into the bed.

I sat up on the edge of the bed and rubbed the sleep out of my eyes. Amber stretched and opened her eyes. We'd hooked up a few times, and once I was ready to call it at night, I'd asked her to come over. She had bright blonde hair and fake tits. She was nowhere near as beautiful as the woman I'd seen at the blackjack table, but she was better than nothing.

"God, I'm sore," Amber said, her voice filled with sleep. I bet. I'd fucked her last night like I was angry. Completely exhausting myself was the only way I was going to get to sleep.

"You should leave before I get out of the shower. If you take anything, I'll know, so don't try it," I warned her before getting up and going to the en suite bathroom. I turned the shower water on and let it run over my sore muscles. It seemed like my body was always sore, not from working out, but from my inability to relax. I was always going from one place to the next, and when I was at home, I wasn't alone. I complained about sore muscles, but I'd rather be completely exhausted than bored.

I got out of the shower and came out of the bathroom. To my surprise, Amber had actually listened, which meant she was using me just as much as I was using her. Maybe I'll hit her up more often since we have an understanding. The bedroom door was open, so Bello was now sitting on my bed. The dog's giant tail hit against the mattress as he wagged it.

I smiled at the big guy. I've had Bello for a few years now. My mom gave me Bello as a gift. She thought it would make me slow down and be home more. To a certain extent, it did. I started to feel guilty if I was away from home for too long. Sometimes, I dropped him off at a dog day care if I was going to be gone for a while. He loved other dogs, so it wasn't a problem. I also hired a dog walker to get Bello as needed.

"Can I get dressed first, big guy?" I asked the dog.

Bello tilted his head to the side and I laughed. I pulled on a pair of jogging pants and a T-shirt before walking into the kitchen. Bello followed behind me. I fed him before grabbing a bowl of cereal for myself. My apartment was the on the top floor of the nicest building I could find in the area. I liked to stay close to my crew as much as possible. Each capo was in charge of a different part of New York. I'd drawn the unlucky straw and gotten the Bronx. Crime was high, which meant I had a lot of competition when it came to drugs and my businesses. I had to compete with a lot of lower-level street thugs and organizations.

Once I was done with my food, I grabbed the leash from the hook on the wall and attached it to Bello's collar. He licked my face as I bent down to attach the leash. We took the elevator down to the bottom floor and walked out the lobby door. The street traffic had slowed a bit, so we were able to walk without worrying about bumping into anyone. Leaves rustled over the concrete, and Bello watched the squirrels as they climbed up the trees and chased each other. He wouldn't go after them. He was good like that. I made sure to take him to training classes as soon as I could. I didn't have time to deal with an untrained animal when there was already so much on my plate. Bello was the friendliest dog I'd ever seen, but he could also attack you at the slightest command from me. I reached in my pocket and pulled out my phone to call the two shitheads from last night to let them know to meet me in an hour. They both must have been asleep when they answered the phone because their voices were groggy. Part of my job as a capo was keeping my crew in line. At the end of the day, the goal was to make money and keep respect. That couldn't happen if my men were ready to kill each other. Bello led me around a couple of blocks before heading back to the apartment. I left a Kong for the dog before going out again to deal with these idiots. The life of a capo never quit, but I was starting to get tired.

Chapter Four

Raven

I took a deep breath before taking the stairs down to the underground gambling ring. Last night didn't turn out how I'd expected. I was beyond rusty. Could barely remember my own hand, let alone try to figure out what other people might have. And it didn't help that I'd snapped at the man who apparently owned the whole place. He was attractive, and maybe if we had met under different circumstances, I would have indulged him. But even then, it wouldn't have led to anything. Men couldn't be trusted. That's how I ended up owning a brothel that was deep in debt to the Irish mafia.

The brightness from the streetlights above dimmed the further I descended the stairs.

The last thing I wanted to do was draw attention to myself tonight, but I knew that was going to be impossible. Last night, the place had been filled with men, and they all looked at me like a dog drooling over a piece of steak. If I wasn't so fucking desperate, I would have never come back. But every time I walked into the house and talked with my girls, I felt guilty. I would not fail them.

"Buy in?" the man at the door asked. He was built like a house, and I'd bet money he was used as the muscle if there was a problem.

I dug in my purse and pulled out the wadded cash. That was another issue. I was going to run out of money fast if I didn't start winning at least a few hands. I had to at least break even each night until I got better at counting. Then, I could go home with the thirty thousand I needed and never see this place again. It sounded good in my head, but I was just hoping that it would actually work.

The man at the door moved to the side to let me past. The underground was dark with just enough light so that I could see the outlines of the tables and the bar. It was hard to make out any exact features of anyone unless I was sitting right beside them—like the guy I met last night. He was handsome. His short hair curled slightly at the top, but the sides were buzzed. He was clean-shaven, and something about him screamed money. It could have been the nice watch he had on or the small gold chain that rested against his caramel skin. He'd been arrogant. I guess he was allowed to be that cocky if he really did own the place.

I wondered what life would be like if I'd gone down the straight and narrow path. Found a normal job, went to college, maybe had a family. I definitely wouldn't be sharpening my card counting skills, surrounded by men who couldn't stop staring at my exposed legs.

I sat down at a blackjack table, just like the night before. The place wasn't as packed today as it had been last night. Two of the men at the table were dressed nicely in button-down shirts while another one had a five-o'clock shadow and bags under his eyes. I kept an eye on him. After working at the brothel so long, I knew when someone was coming down from a bender.

"You in?" the dealer asked. Unlike at the casino, the dealer was dressed in jeans and a black T-shirt. His gun was holstered on his hip as a silent warning.

"Yes." I reached in my purse, counted out the money, and gave it to the dealer. He counted it again and then added it to the pile. He dealt the cards and I got down to work.

Counting cards came down to one thing: assigning a number to the high and low cards and using that to identify my chances of winning. The idea is to bet low when chances of winning are low and bet high when chances of winning were high, but since I was trying to hone my skills, I wasn't paying much attention to my bet strategy yet.

The hard part was keeping track of the number each player had and remembering if it was to my advantage or not. I used to be great at it a long time ago. I could talk and drink all while keeping the cards straight in my head, but now I had to really concentrate without being obvious. No matter what, it would take a few hands for me to get into the flow.

I lost the first hand but couldn't afford to lose another, but I was able to win some of my money back during the second hand. After about five rounds and a couple more people joining the table, I started to remember all the tricks and tips I used to use. I was nowhere near as good as I used to be, but I was getting there.

When I looked up at the big clock hanging over the bar, I realized I'd been sitting in the same spot for three hours. I lost a little bit of money but still had enough to get in next time. Deciding to call it a night, I stuffed my winnings into my bag and walked over to the bar.

Might as well get a drink before going back to the brothel and working for a little bit. I pulled myself onto a barstool and ordered a rum and Coke. As I waited for the bartender to fix up my drink, I looked around the room.

Leaning against the end of the bar talking with another guy was the man from last night. He nodded as he listened to the guy in front of him speak. I didn't miss the way his eyes flickered to me. I quickly turned my head.

The bartender set the drink in front of me. I took a sip, and a moment later, the man slid into the stool next to me. Fuck.

"Came back for more?" he asked. His voice was deep, and it sent a shiver down my spine.

Tonight, he was dressed in dark jeans and a blue button-down shirt. With the light coming from the bar, I could see his muscles rippling underneath his shirt. His green eyes roamed over my body. Most of the time, I hated when men looked at me like that, but with him, knowing he was checking me out, a spark of excitement lit up in my chest. His tongue grazed over his bottom lip. That might have just been the sexiest thing I've ever seen.

"I'm here for the game," I said, finding my voice.

He turned to face the bar and ordered a shot of cognac. I drank my rum and Coke while waiting for the bartender to make his drink. He raised his shot glass to my glass and clinked them together before shooting it back. He didn't make a face or show that the shot affected him at all. It reminded me of one of my foster parents who'd been an angry drunk. Drank the shit like water.

"So, what really brings you hear? You're not my typical customer."

"Why? Because I'm not a man?" I asked, proud of myself for being able to talk in complete sentences as he stared at me.

"Precisely."

I didn't answer because I wasn't sure what to tell him. I didn't expect anyone to question my reason for being at the underground. I just needed to build up my skills and then get away with enough money to pay off the Irish. After that, I never wanted to come back to this place again. I sipped my drink, faster now, so I could get far away from this man.

He scooted his barstool closer to me so that our legs were almost touching. Goosebumps rose over my skin in anticipation. It had been a long time since I allowed a man to touch me. My body was begging for him to reach his hand out to rest on my bare leg.

I needed to get it together. I was about to steal from his pockets. I couldn't let my body betray me. He put an elbow on the bar and leaned close to me. The smell of his cologne and the cognac filled my nose.

"How about we go back to my place for the night?" he asked. My jaw nearly dropped in shock. Well, that was bold! If he was ballsy enough to proposition a woman he barely knew, it was probably a common occurrence for him, and I had no desire to be another notch on his bedpost.

I downed the rest of my drink. "I don't even know your name."

"Enzo."

Enzo. It sounded just as dark and dangerous as he looked. "I have to be at work," I said.

He looked up at the clock on the wall and raised an eyebrow. "Now?"

I smiled at him. "You aren't the only one working in the dead of night."

"Where do you work?" he asked.

I debated if I should tell him or not. If he found out I'd been counting cards, he'd be able to track me down. I didn't answer.

"Beautiful woman who only comes out at the dead of night and plays blackjack at a place like this? I'm guessing you aren't an overnight nurse? Stripper?" he guessed.

I raised an eyebrow at him. "You think I'm a stripper?"

He looked over my body one more time. "You're too pretty to be a stripper, but that's my best guess."

"And what do you do?" I asked.

He sat up in the chair and looked around the room. "This...and other things."

"That's vague."

"How about you come home with me and I'll tell you more about what I do? You can tell me more about what you do. It will be a fun time."

His words were almost enough for me to say "fuck it" and follow the man home. What are the chances he'd even care enough about me afterwards to bother seeing if I was counting cards? But I couldn't risk it. I thought about my girls back at the brothel. I couldn't gamble with their lives like that.

"Maybe next time," I told him before standing from the barstool. His eyes burned a hole in my back as I walked out the door. Once I got up the stairs, the cool autumn air surrounded me. I took a deep breath, clearing my nose of the stuffiness of the gambling room. The street was nearly empty like it usually was at this time at night, but of course, the stores were all open. New York never slept. I'd only taken a few steps when I felt cold metal press against my scalp. My body froze. Ice ran through my veins.

"I'm not going to hurt you," a dark voice said from behind me. My eyes searched the street, but no one was around. I was hidden enough in the shadows that if someone walked by, they might not even see me. I had a gun in my purse, but there was no way I'd be able to get to it. At least not before he pulled the trigger.

"Slide your purse off your shoulder slowly and hand it to me," he commanded. Fuck, fuck, fuck. Why hadn't I been more careful? I was usually so aware of my surroundings. I took a deep breath and started to reach for the strap of my purse. All my gambling money was in this purse. If I didn't have money to play with next time, then I was screwed with the Irish.

My hand moved closer to the base of the purse. If I could move fast enough maybe I could get the gun. It was a risky move, but if I let this man take all my money, I'd have no chance of paying back my debt. They'd take my girls and sell them to some sick bastard.

"Now!" the man yelled as the gun shook in his hand. I could feel it move against my head.

"I'd put that down if I were you," a familiar voice said from behind the robber. I wanted to turn around to see, but I was still too scared to move. One twitch of the man's finger, and my brains would be all over the sidewalk.

"Mind your business!" the robber snapped. "Give me the purse!"

His hand shook even harder as he grew impatient. The sound of a grunt filled my ears, and the metal against my head was snatched away. I turned around fast to see that Enzo had wrestled the man to the ground. The gun clattered to the sidewalk and slid toward me. I could pick it up, but from what I could tell, Enzo had it handled. His knee was in the man's back as the man squirmed, trying to get free.

Enzo turned to me. "Go back to the underground and grab the man at the door," he said his voice surprisingly calm, considering he just took down a robber. I didn't need to be told twice. I ran back down the steps to the underground.

"Enzo is upstairs and needs your help," I sputtered to the security guy standing at the door with his arms crossed over his chest. His eyes widened, and he followed me up the steps to the sidewalk. Enzo had managed to pull the attacker up to his feet and hold him against the light post. The security guard rushed to his side and took Enzo's place.

"Get rid of this guy. He's out here robbing women in the middle of the night like a fucking coward," Enzo said to his security. He straightened his shirt and walked toward me. The cocky grin on his lips from only minutes ago at the bar was gone. His fingers brushed my elbow.

"Are you okay?" he asked. His eyes glistened under the lamp pole.

There was a dangerous man underneath that cockiness. A man who could easily take down someone with a gun and then act like it wasn't a big deal.

I nodded. "I'm fine...thank you."

He looked me over as if not sure if he believed my words.

"I'll walk you home," he said.

I started shaking my head. "You don't—"

"It wasn't a question."

I was taken back by his bluntness. "I'll be fine—"

He turned and started walking away from me. I had to jog to keep up.

"Hey, I was talking to you," I snapped. I was grateful that he'd stepped in when he did, but I couldn't show him where I lived.

"Left or right?" he asked as we came to a crosswalk.

"Are you listening to me?"

"I can get on the phone and find out everything about you in a matter of seconds. If you don't tell where you live so I can make sure you get home safety, I'll figure it out."

I searched his eyes, looking to see if he was bluffing. Part of being a good card-counter was being able to read people. There was no waver in his expression. He was telling the truth. I didn't know who Enzo really was, but I was starting to get the feeling he was a more powerful man than I'd thought.

"Right." I swallowed the lump in my throat.

I walked next him in the direction of the brothel. At least this way, he wouldn't know my home address. He couldn't catch me while I was sleeping. We walked the entire way in silence. Masculine, dangerous energy surrounded us. It was rolling off of him in waves. I just had to be careful not to get swept up in it. No one had ever saved me; not one person had ever stuck up for me like Enzo had.

When I stopped in front of the building, he raised an eyebrow. "No way."

"What?" I asked, looking around like I was missing something.

"There's no way you're a prostitute," he said matter-of-factly. Of course he would know that this wasn't a regular house. Did this man know all the shady businesses in New York?

I smiled at him. "And why not?"

He scoffed and ran a hand over his smooth jawline. "I know prostitutes, and you aren't one."

Does that mean he paid for prostitutes? I couldn't imagine a man that looked like him needing to pay money for someone to have sex with him. I thought about lying. Maybe that would get him to leave me alone.

"I own the brothel," I said, the truth slipping from my lips.

His eyes widened in surprised, and he crossed his arms over his chest before a mischievous look crossed his face. "You own a brothel?"

"Yes. Is there something wrong with that?" I waited for him to laugh in my face.

"No, it's actually pretty impressive."

We stared at each other for a moment. I wasn't sure what to say. That's the last thing I expected to come out of his mouth. Most people looked down on my business. No one really knew how hard it was to run a brothel, especially as a woman.

"I should probably go inside," I said, breaking the tension.

"What's your name?" he asked.

"Raven."

He nodded. "I'll see you around, Raven."

Chapter Five

I spotted Toby immediately. He was behind the bar tonight, leaning across it and flirting with a blonde on the other side.

"I'm gonna grab a drink," Erica said from behind me, before walking to an empty spot at the counter. She'd decided to take the night off and come with me to meet Toby.

I had questions for him. I shouldn't have blindly followed his idea to start counting cards again. I needed to know how deep of shit I was in.

I sat in one of the stools and waited for Toby to notice me. Once he did, he stood up straight and walked over.

"What's up?"

"Can we talk?" I asked. He looked around the bar and waved a hand at the other bartender, letting her know he was stepping out for a minute. He rounded the bar, and I met him at the end before we both walked outside. Toby rummaged in his pocket before pulling out a cigarette and putting it in between his lips.

"What's going on?" he asked. He rounded his hands around the end of the cigarette to keep out the wind as he lit it.

"Who owns the underground gambling spot that you sent me to?" I'd been thinking about the question for the last couple days. The last two times I went back to the underground, I hadn't seen Enzo. The move he pulled the other night told me he was dangerous, but I wanted to know exactly who I was dealing with before stealing from him.

Toby took a drag of the cigarette before blowing out a puff of smoke. "Why? Just get your money and get out of there. Don't spend too much time lingering."

"Yeah, it's a little too late for that. I'm rusty. I've been there for a week trying to sharpen my skills."

Toby ran a hand through his hair. "Fuck, Raven. Couldn't you have practiced at the casino?"

"It's not the same." I didn't feel like explaining to him how I needed to be comfortable in the place before I bet that much money. I needed to be able to read the room and know the other players. "Who owns it?" I asked again.

"The mob." He searched my eyes for some kind of response. A chill ran down my spine. That wasn't the answer I wanted. I was hoping it was owned by some low-level street gang. It obviously wasn't the Irish mob he was talking about, or they would have already dragged me out of there, which left only one option. It was owned by the most powerful people in New York city. They were above all other criminals, even above the police in some cases. The Italian mob had a lot of people on their payroll, and nobody stole from the mob unless they were willing to risk their life.

"You sent me to steal from a mob establishment?" I whisper-screamed at him, suddenly furious. Heat filled my face. I was probably as bright as a tomato.

"Shhh. I didn't know you were going to hang around there. You were just supposed to count cards, win your cash, and get out."

"That's not how it works. Don't you think it would have been even more suspicious if someone who has never been in there before walks in and wins big?"

His eyebrows furrowed together. I ran a hand over my face. This was so much worse than I'd thought.

"Okay, calm down—"

"Don't tell me to calm down. I'm the one putting my life at risk!"

"Your life is at risk either way."

I turned away from him and started to pace the sidewalk in front of the bar. What was I going to do? It was too late to just disappear. I *had* to get the money. Toby was right. Either way, I was risking my life. How had I gotten stuck between two criminal organizations when all I wanted to do was run my business?

Toby took another drag of his cigarette. "Listen, I know you're in deep shit right now—"

I snorted. "Ya think?"

He blew out a puff of smoke. "But let's just get it over with. Like ripping off a Band-Aid. You only need one big win, and then you can pay off the Irish and put all this shit behind you. They'll just think you got lucky and you were smart and didn't keep playing."

I stopped my pacing and leaned my head against the cool window of the bar. "I'm so fucked."

Chapter Six

<u>Enzo</u>

"How much for the three on this block?" I asked Tom, my real estate agent. We stood on the sidewalk of one of the worst neighborhoods in the Bronx. Tom looked like he was going to shit himself.

"Three-hundred thousand for all of them. They are in pretty bad shape right now..."

I looked at the three buildings in front of us. They were all brick, and two of them were boarded up. The lawns were overgrown, and an abandoned tricycle was left flipped over and forgotten in the small alleyway between the buildings. I wouldn't be surprised if there were a few homeless people who squatted inside during the cold winter months.

"I'll take them," I said without hesitation. I didn't need any additional ways to clean my money, but if I did, this was a great way to do it. I wanted to restore some of the rough neighborhoods. It wasn't something I had to do, and sometimes, I questioned why I even wasted my time. There was a good chance the houses would just get trashed again. I'd already bought five houses on the next block over, and every time I put new windows in, a drive-by shooting would take them out. I was starting to think that the neighbors had a personal vendetta against me.

"Do you want to come by the office and talk about loans?" Tom asked.

I shook my head and stepped around Tom to open my car door. I'd decided to leave the Lamborghini at home for this trip. I wasn't scared of anyone trying me. I think it's rude to flash around my wealth when so many people in this area were going without the necessities. I reached into the back of the car and grabbed a duffle bag. I threw it to Tom, who took a step back with the impact. I paid the guy a lot of money to handle the buying process without a lot of interaction from me. With everything else going on in my life, I didn't have time to worry about these projects as much. Once everything was finished, I'd have contractors come in and let me know if any of the houses were salvageable, or if it was better to completely tear them down and start over from scratch.

"Let me know once everything is finalized so I can get my contractors over here," I told him.

Tom nodded and, with the bag in hand, quickly walked to his car.

I stayed and watched to make sure he didn't get robbed before turning to my own vehicle. I paused with my hand on the door handle when I noticed the five men standing on the other side of the street. They all had snares on their face.

"Problem?" I asked, my voice filled with annoyance.

"You buying these homes like you're from here," onc of the men said, taking a step forward. I could see the gun clearly tucked into the waistband of his jeans. He wore a white beater and red basketball shorts. He must have been the leader of the group.

I almost laughed at their appearance. They were nothing compared to the power of Cosa Nostra, but they could still cause problems that I wanted no part of.

"If you have an issue with it, you know where to find me," I said before getting in the car and driving off. The small street gangs were going to be a problem. They didn't like change, especially in a neighborhood where they made a lot of money off people who bought drugs over groceries. I kept my crew off their territory and they stayed off mine, but the gangs were starting to look at me buying these houses as an attack. The last thing I wanted right now was more problems, but the project was already underway. Hopefully, they wouldn't be stupid enough to make a move.

*****

I jogged down the steps to the underground and almost ran smack-dab into Raven. I caught her arms to steady her. "Whoa there."

She gave me a forced smile. "Oh, hey Enzo."

She was dressed more casually each time I saw her. Today, she wore tight jeans and a flowy top. Her long red hair was pulled up into a big bun on top of her head. I would have never guessed that she ran a brothel just by looking at her. It scared me to think of her being the only protection between a man and one of the women. I didn't know much about brothels, but I figured it was a pretty dangerous business to run. It was the only illegal business I hadn't gotten myself involved in.

I cleared my throat. "Going to work?"

"Yeah, I was just going to grab some coffee first."

"I'll come with you," I said. I wasn't sure why I offered. There was business to take care of at the underground, but going to get coffee with Raven seemed more important. I wanted to know more about her. How did someone so beautiful and put together end up running a brothel? What was her story? She opened her mouth, probably to tell me to get lost.

"Just in case you get robbed again," I added. God, I sounded lame. I hadn't hooked up with anyone since the first night I'd seen Raven walk into the door of my gambling room. I'd been working from sunup to sundown, so I hadn't been in the mood to call up Amber or any other of my regular fuck buddies.

Raven bit down on her lip. "Fine, come on." She turned around to start walking.

"Let me drive," I offered. She hesitated for a second. "If I was trying to kidnap you, I would have done it the other night."

"Fine, but I don't normally get in cars with men I don't know."

"Good to know."

I started walking the other way toward my car, and she followed behind me. I was parked down the street in a well-lit area. I pulled my keys out from my pocket and pressed the unlock button. The lights on the car lit up.

"No fucking way," she said.

I turned around to see that her eyes had widened to the size of saucers. I smiled at her. I was used to getting that reaction when I brought out the Lamborghini. I had a small collection of really nice cars, but the Lambo was my favorite.

"Come on." I moved around the car to open the passenger door for her. She strode slowly toward the car as if scared to get close. "It doesn't bite."

She rolled her eyes. "I know that."

She slid onto the red leather seat, and I closed the door before rounding the car to get in on my side.

"I guess the underground does well?" She asked once we were on the road.

"That, and a few other businesses."

If she hasn't figured out that the underground is owned by the mafia, I wasn't going to be the one to tell her.

"Where is this place?" I asked.

"Oh, make a left."

I turned the wheel. The streets were empty at this time. The only people out were ones like me and Raven, people who lived on the wrong side of the law.

"Make a right."

I did as she said, the Lamborghini smoothly taking each turn.

"It's coming up right here on the corner."

It wasn't a coffee shop, but a small diner with a big red clock hanging on the outside. I parked out front and rounded the car to open her door, but she was already getting out.

"You come here a lot?" I asked, trying to get a better picture of her. She was a mystery to me. If she owned the brothel, she had to be bringing in money, so why was she gambling it away at the underground? She wasn't winning anything. I'd asked my bookkeeper; she was barely breaking even.

"I've gotten to know the owner real well. He's a nice guy," she said, leading me into the diner. The door chimed as we walked inside. The place needed an upgrade, but it also had a homey feel to it. Pictures lined the walls of what must have been their grand opening. In one picture, a man stood in front of the bar with his arm around a smiling woman. Just from the photo, I could tell they were in love. It was the same kind of love I remembered my mom and dad having before he passed away. A love so strong, you could see it, even in print.

"How's it going, Raven?" a man said from behind the counter. He was the older version of the man from the picture. His hair was graying. He wiped down the counter with a rag.

"How's it going, Elmo?" Raven seated herself at a booth. I took the seat across from her.

"Just keeping busy. The usual?" the man asked her as he tucked the rag under the counter and turned around to wash his hands.

"Just a coffee."

The man dried his hands and walked to the front of the counter. "How about you?" He turned to face me.

"I'll have a coffee too. Thank you."

The man nodded and started to brew a fresh pot of coffee. The smell filled the small diner, covering the previous scent of burgers and fries.

I focused my attention back on Raven. "I'm guessing you come here a lot?"

She nodded, causing a piece of her long red hair to come out of the bun and land on her shoulder. Her hair was so long and thick, it was a mystery how she'd gotten it up so high on her head. I preferred it down so I could imagine wrapping my hands around it. She didn't look like the usual girls I hooked up with. Something about her was different, exotic.

She lifted an eyebrow, having caught me staring, and I shifted in my seat. The man returned with two steaming mugs.

"Thanks, Elmo," she said.

"Let me know if you need anything else." Elmo walked away, leaving us alone at the booth.

She pulled the organizer that held creamer and sugar packet toward her and instantly started dumping a hefty amount of creamer into the coffee.

"Holy shit, do you even want to taste the coffee?"

She smiled. "I have a bit of a sweet tooth." She set the creamer down and started opening up packets of sugar.

I pulled my coffee mug up to my mouth and took a sip. The hot liquid warmed my throat as I continued to watch her pour sugar into her mug. She grabbed a spoon and stirred her coffee.

"So how does someone like you come to own a brothel?" I asked, coming straight out with the question that's been on my mind since the moment I found out.

"How did you come to own an underground gambling spot?" She cocked an eyebrow, taking a drink of her caffeinated syrup.

"You first."

She took another sip of her coffee. I couldn't help noticing the way her plump lips balanced on the side of the coffee cup. I wondered how they'd feel against my cock. She swallowed and set the cup down on the table.

"I worked a lot of...odd jobs and saved up enough money to buy the brothel from someone who I thought was a friend of mine. The rest is kind of history," she said, picking the cup back up.

"But why would a girl like you want to own a brothel?"

"What do you mean a girl like me?" she asked, her face twisted up like she was actually confused by the question.

"There's a story in there somewhere," I pushed.

She shrugged. "Maybe. Or maybe the brothel just brings in money that I desperately needed at the time. It's a very profitable business. Men pay ridiculous amounts of money just to get their dick sucked by a woman that could care less if they walked outside and got hit by a car. It's kind of sad, actually. Most of the men don't even take off their wedding rings when they come in."

I took a moment to let her words sink in. Most people would feel sad for the women in that situation, thinking they are being taken advantage of, but instead, she felt sorry for the men and the men's wives. Maybe she had a skewered view of men. She wouldn't be entirely wrong.

"Your turn. How did you come to own an underground gambling place?" she asked.

"I guess you could say I was born into the business. I have my hands in a little bit of everything: real estate, gambling, guns, drugs...actually, I think the only thing I don't have in my portfolio is prostitution."

She smirked. "It's good business to be in. So, with all this going on, when do you sleep?"

I laughed. "I don't, really."

The look on her face wasn't one of admiration or shock but, instead, a look of sadness, like she pitied me. It was the same look on my mother's face when she told me that I worked too hard. I hated that look.

I cleared my throat and shifted uncomfortably in the booth. I brought the coffee cup to my lips and drank the last of it, allowing the liquid to burn my throat as it went down.

I wasn't usually a coffee drinker, but I was discovering I'd follow this woman anywhere. I wanted to spend more time with her, even it was just to sit across from her and marvel at her beauty.

"You're staring again," she said.

I smiled. "Am I?"

"You do that a lot."

I shrugged. "Maybe I like what I see."

Her cheeks turned a rosy color, and she grabbed her cup of coffee to try to hide her discomfort. I loved the way her cheeks reddened like that. I still couldn't picture her running a brothel surrounded by dirty men who had to pay to get their dick wet.

She finished her coffee and set the empty mug down on the table. I grabbed my wallet and left a twenty on the table.

"Work?" I asked.

"Yeah."

We stood up from the stool and walked out to my car.

*****

The brothel looked like any other building on the street. It blended in nicely with the neighborhood. I reached for the door handle to get out.

"Uh, what are you doing?" she asked.

"Walking you to the door."

"I think I can manage," she said as she stepped out of the car. I got out behind her.

"Are you sure? Because last time, you only took a few steps away from the underground before you were held at gun point."

She flipped me the bird, and I laughed as I walked behind her up the steps to the front door.

The door flung open just as Raven reached for the handle. A girl that looked to be maybe nineteen with dark, wild hair stood in the foyer. Her face was red and her eyebrows drew together.

"He got handsy…he's upstairs with Erica. I tried—" the girl gushed. Before she got the whole story out, Raven brushed past the girl and grabbed a metal baseball bat that was leaning next to the entrance. I followed behind her as she ran up the wooden stairs to the top floor. There had be at least seven rooms up here, all of them right next to each other.

"What the fuck did I say?!" a male voice yelled from the end of hall. I grabbed the Desert Eagle that I always kept in the waistband of my jeans and held it out in front of me, pointed at the floor.

"Get the fuck off of me, you piece of shit," a women's voice replied to the man. Raven pulled back the curtain to one of the rooms. A man about six feet tall with a big beer belly held a woman against the wall. One of his hands clenched around her throat while the other one was under her skirt.

"She said, get off of her," Raven barked. The man turned to look at Raven with a sick smile on his face.

"Come on, Princess, don't—"

Bang!

The man fell to the floor with a thud. The women screamed. Her half-naked body and face were covered in blood

Raven turned on me as I tucked the gun back into my waistband.

"You fucking killed him!" she shouted. To my surprise, she didn't seem overly sickened by the sight of a man dying right in front of her. Instead, she balled her hands into fist as if I was the one attacking one of her girls.

"Someone was going to have to. It's good to set an example," I replied.

"Oh my god, oh my god," the woman repeated over and over again as her body shook. "I'm going to be sick."

"Holy shit," I heard from behind me. Five other women were standing in the doorway, their eyes on the dead body. Raven walked further inside the bedroom and grabbed the blood-covered woman. Raven led her across the hall to what I assumed was a bathroom.

"Stay here," she seethed at me before shutting the bathroom door.

I bent down to the man's body and checked his pulse, just to be sure. He was dead alright. I'd shot him straight through the head. The sound of feet shuffling across the hardwood floor echoed against the walls as the women retreated.

How often did shit like this happen? Prostitution wasn't an easy industry, and to think that Raven had been running this by herself put a knot in my stomach. She needed someone to protect these girls; she couldn't do it by herself with a metal baseball bat. I pulled out my phone and called Charles.

"Boss," Charles answered.

"I need a clean-up crew at the brothel off of Moorside Path."

"I'm on it." He hung up the phone.

I stood up from my crouched position and took a look around the room. It wasn't very big, just a full-sized bed, a dresser, and a couple of bookshelves that didn't hold any actual books. Instead, it was filled with small containers for storage. I didn't have much experience with brothels, but from my understanding, they were usually in much worse condition.

The women usually didn't even have the bare necessities, let alone a nice room to themselves.

The curtain was pulled back, and Raven stepped through into the bedroom again. She looked just as pissed off as she was before she left with the woman. I had to admit, angry Raven was hot. Her cheeks matched that bright red hair of hers, and her lips were curled into a snarl. My dick twitched at the sight.

"You fucking killed one of my customers!" she snapped.

"What was I supposed to do?"

"I had it handled."

"What? With a baseball bat? What if he had a gun on him? You need someone here to watch over the girls—"

"I watch over the girls, and I don't need the mafia stepping in," she said.

Ah, so she did know the underground was run by Cosa Nostra. I stared at her, amazed by her stubbornness. I didn't want to think about what could have happened if I hadn't been here.

"Can you just go?"

"My guys will be here to clean everything up. Just leave the body where it is," I said before walking past her and out to my car.

Chapter Seven

I sat at the desk and counted the money in the safe. I hadn't gone to the underground in a couple days. I was still pissed at Enzo for coming in here and killing a guy, and then telling me how to run my business. I haven't needed anyone else in a long time, and I wasn't going to need anyone now. If the Irish taught me anything, it was that getting the mafia involved only meant making problems worse. I was also shaken by how quick Enzo was to shoot someone. He didn't hesitate or try to de-escalate the situation. Is that what would happen to me if he found out I was cheating? Would he shoot me right between the eyes without a second thought? A chill ran over my body the more I thought about it.

"You leaving tonight?" Erica asked as she leaned against the desk.

"I don't know."

"Go. We'll be fine. You've barely left this place in two days. We can handle things here for a few hours. Just go get your money."

I stayed quiet, continuing to count the money in my hand.

"Is this because of that big sexy man who came in here guns blazing? You're scared of him?"

"Wouldn't you be?" I asked, looking up from the handful of money.

"Not if I knew him."

"What do you mean?" I put the money down, giving Erica my full attention.

"What do you think I mean? Can't you do with him the same thing we do here? Get to know him, seduce him, do what you gotta do so that he won't even notice or care when you take $30,000 from him."

I scoffed. "I think he'd know." He wasn't stupid.

Erica shrugged. "Well, then, maybe he won't care."

It was far-fetched, but I had thought about it before. Could Enzo be manipulated enough that he wouldn't come after me once I took the $30,000 and disappeared? Could I convince him that I just got really lucky one night and didn't want to gamble it away?

I sat back in the office chair. "Do you think we need help around here...ya know, like protection?"

"Honestly? Yeah. I think it would make the girls feel a lot better if we had a little more than a baseball bat."

I sighed. Maybe Enzo was right. Maybe I was naive thinking I could keep all the girls safe by myself.

"Listen, if you don't want to hire someone or get anyone involved in your business, I understand. The Irish have caused enough trouble for us anyway."

I grabbed the money from the safe and stuffed it into my purse. "I'll be back in a few hours," I told Erica as I stood up.

Erica waved at me. "We'll be fine. Go get your money."

*****

The underground was packed tonight. There weren't any seats open at the blackjack table, so I sat at the bar and had a drink while waiting for something to open up. I sensed his presence before even turning around. He was dressed in a three-piece suit, like a true businessman. His watch glistened in the dim lights from above. I loved that I had his full attention and I didn't even have to do anything to get it. I grabbed my drink and took a sip, keeping my eyes on him as he crossed the room.

"You still mad at me?" he asked, his voice deep. It must be the alcohol that was making my body feel so warm.

"A little bit," I admitted.

"You aren't playing tonight?"

"I'm waiting for a table to open up."

He looked around the room as if just noticing that the place was completely packed. "Give me a minute."

He walked over to the blackjack table and leaned down to talk to one of the men at the table. The man nodded quickly and took his money before standing up from the table and walking away. He smiled at me and waved me over. I rolled my eyes, downed the rest of my drink, and then took the spot the man had left.

"Really? Bullying people?" I asked.

"It's kind of what I do."

The front door closed and Enzo turned his head. I followed his line of sight to a man that was also dressed in a suit.

"Find me before you leave. I have some business to take care of," he told me before walking away from the table and slapping hands with the man at the door.

"Are you in, Miss?" the dealer asked.

"Sorry, yes." I grabbed the money out of my purse and added to the pile. The game started, and I stayed focused for the next few hours. People came and went, but I stayed in the same spot. My counting skills were good enough to go for the $30,000. I was currently up $1,000, but I didn't want to keep pushing my luck. Enzo would know something was up if I walked away with $30,000 right now. It was too risky. I folded my cards and took my winnings. My body hurt from sitting too long. Standing to stretch, I spotted Enzo across the room. Like always, his eyes were focused on me, even as he talked with the bartender.

Coffee? He mouthed to me. I smiled and nodded. He said something to the bartender before coming toward me. We walked out to his car.

"Oh, shit," he said, looking at the clock on the dashboard.

"What?"

"We got to make a quick stop." He pulled away from the curb.

"Um...okay."

"I have to let my dog out."

I almost laughed, thinking he was joking. "Really?"

"Yeah, my dog walker is out of town this week and I didn't put him in day care." His eyes flickered to me. "What's so funny?"

"Nothing, it's just...kind of cute."

He rolled his eyes. "The other night, I was a murderer. Now I'm cute?"

I shrugged. "I guess you're a complex man."

He pulled into a parking garage, and I followed him across the lot to the elevator. It took us up to the top floor and opened into a short hallway. There were only two doors on this floor. He walked to the second one and inserted a key. The place was huge for a New York apartment. It wasn't luxurious like I'd pictured. It had a more rustic look to it. There was a large wooden dining room table to the left. On the right was the kitchen area with dark wooden cabinets. I didn't get a chance to take in anymore of the space because a giant dog came running straight for me.

"Bello!" Enzo yelled, trying to control the dog, but it was too late. He jumped up, landing his paws on my stomach and almost knocking me over. I would have been scared if it wasn't for the wagging tail and his tongue sticking out the side of his mouth.

I laughed and rubbed a hand over the dog's head. "Well, hello there."

Enzo grabbed the dog by the collar to peel him off of me. "I'm sorry about that. He's usually better behaved. He must like you."

I waved it off. "It's fine."

He let go of the dog's collar and grabbed a blue leash from the hook on the wall. He clipped it to the collar.

"Ready?" he asked.

"Yep." I opened the door and let Enzo led the way. I followed them to the elevator. The dog kept turning around to look at me.

"Bello, you act like you've never saw a woman before," Enzo said to the dog.

"Not a woman like me," I said as I bent down to pet Bello's head.

We walked out to the empty sidewalk and started down the street with Bello between the two of us.

"So, do you always walk him at two in the morning?" I asked.

He shook his head. "I usually have someone who walks him during the day, but she's on vacation."

"You don't have family who can watch him?" I shouldn't pry. It was none of my business anyways, but maybe the more I knew about him, the more leverage I'd have. We stopped as Bello sniffed a tree.

"I'm an only child. I have cousins, but they're busy most of the time. Some of them are involved in the mob, so they don't have the time," he explained. That was more family then I had. I wondered what it was like to have parents and cousins to visit on holidays.

"What about you?" he asked as we started walking again. He allowed Bello to control the walk as we turned the corner and passed by a group of girls who looked like they were on their way home from a nightclub.

"No family. I grew up in foster care...well, except for Toby. He's like a brother to me."

"I'm sorry," he said. I looked up to see him staring at me. Instead of the usual look of pity I got from people when I told them my history, it was a sincere apology, as if he was somehow responsible.

I shrugged. "It's okay. It was a long time ago."

I tried not to think about my time in foster care. Some of the foster homes I lived in were just terrible. I saw things that no child should ever see, and there was never anyone there to protect me. No one ever shielded me from adult life the way that kids were supposed to be shielded. Not until I moved in with Toby's family. They were genuinely good people. I was there for a couple years, and I thought I'd stay until I turned eighteen, but I messed that up when I got caught selling weed at school. It was a stupid thing to do, but I was glad that Toby had stuck around and stayed in touch with me after the ordeal.

We walked the rest of the way in comfortable silence, stopping occasionally so that Bello could sniff the bushes. When we got back to the apartment, Enzo hung the leash up.

"Do you want to give him a treat?" he offered.

I smiled, liking this softer side of Enzo, especially after he murdered a man. He handed me a small biscuit.

"You have to tell him to sit first," he instructed.

Bello looked up at me, his tail wagging in anticipation.

"Sit," I told the dog. He did as I said, and I threw the treat at him, which he caught midair. I patted him on the head.

When I stood back up, Enzo's eyes were trained on me, dilated wide with desire. I felt it too. The air in the room shifted.

My breath caught in my throat as he stepped close. The smell of his cologne came off his body in waves, filling my nose and the space between us. Was I really going to do this? It wouldn't be the first time I slept with a dangerous man, but I'd never slept with someone as dangerous as Enzo. The mafia ran every inch of this city. I was playing with fire, but the fire was so warm and welcoming, all I wanted to do was fall right into it. Erica's voice replayed in my head. *Seduce him. Do what you gotta do so that he won't even notice or care when you take $30,000 from him.* Bello whined, but when Enzo didn't pay the dog any attention. I listened to the sound of his paws walking across the floor, leaving us in the kitchen. Enzo's eyes were trained on me as if I was the most beautiful woman in the world. It was dirty to have sex with a man I was about to steal from, but right now, nothing felt more right. It was obvious he wanted me. So what if I happened to benefit from it? Would he really turn his head the other way when I took his money if I let him in my panties? I doubted it, but I became too focused on his dark smoldering eyes to care. He placed a hand on the wall next to my head and leaned in close. I clenched my thighs together, trying to get myself under control. I hadn't even looked at a man in months, and here I was, the sole focus of a very powerful and dangerous man.

"I would give anything to kiss you right now," he said, his voice coming out deep and husky. A chill ran down my spine.

"Then kiss me," I encouraged, wanting to feel his lips against my own. I had no doubt that this would be the best kiss I'd ever have. He looked in my eyes, as if searching for any kind of hesitation.

"I won't be able to stop at just a kiss. Are you okay with that?"

I swallowed. I hadn't planned to sleep with him tonight, but now that we were here, I wouldn't be able to walk away. Not when my body felt one-hundred degrees hotter and there's an itch between my legs. He stepped closer to me, pressing his body against mine. The bulge in his pants rubbed against me. He bent his head down, and his warm breath send chills over my skin.

"Say yes," he encouraged. I didn't need any more convincing.

"Yes," I squeaked out.

His lips softly grazed against my neck, and I moaned from the simple contact. I bit down on my lips, embarrassed by the outburst. My sex deprivation was differently showing. But Enzo seemed to like it. His lips lifted into a smile against the crook of my neck. He littered kisses from my neck down to my collarbone. His hand went to my waist, as if to keep me in place, as he trailed his lips down to my cleavage. I clenched my thighs tighter as he moved from my cleavage back up to my face. He stared at me for a beat before pressing his lips to mine. The touch sent an electric shock through my body. I relaxed into it; I had no control over my own senses. I couldn't think straight as his kisses turned more hungry. As if he couldn't get enough. Another moan escaped my lips as his hand moved from my waist to grip my ass. I wrapped my arms around his broad shoulders. He pulled back and searched my eyes. I took a deep breath, trying to calm my nerves as he grabbed my hand and led me through the apartment to a bedroom. The bedroom contained a king-sized bed and dresser, but besides that, it barely looked like it was lived in. I walked past him and sat on the mattress, making myself comfortable. He smiled at me but stayed standing.

"What?" I asked.

"I like the sight of you in my bed."

"Just for tonight...Nothing more," I said with a warning.

I just needed to get in his head a little bit so I could take the money. I didn't need a relationship, especially not with someone in the mob who might be interested in taking part of my brothel. I could handle things on my own, and a relationship meant someone looking over my shoulder.

He stalked toward me and placed both arms on either side of my body. He leaned forward until I laid flat against the mattress. "Whatever you say, baby."

I wanted to correct him and tell him I wasn't his baby but the way the word rolled so easily off his tongue, I let it slide. I ignored the term of endearment and the butterflies that erupted in my stomach. He hovered on top of me as I wrapped my legs around his waist. His movement had pushed my dress up to my stomach.

I grabbed at his jeans, fumbling with the zipper in my haste, until his dick sprain free. My breath caught in my throat as I got a good look at the source of his cockiness. I've seen a lot of penises in my life—most of the times when I didn't want to—but nothing could compare to his. It was thick and much bigger than average. I didn't get a chance to admire it much longer because the sound of material ripping brought me back to the present as Enzo tore my panties.

"I'll buy you some more," he promised.

I nodded but couldn't care less about the ripped material. All I wanted was him. His fingers rubbed against my clit, and I let out a soft moan as my body tingled. I could orgasm right now just from the smallest touch from him.

"Fuck, you're wet," he said as he inserted two fingers inside me. It had been so long, even that made me feel full, and I started to worry about how big he was.

"Shit," I moaned as he rubbed my clit while also keeping the two fingers inside me. I gripped the sheets as my wall tightened. My orgasm builds until I'm right on the edge. Each stroke of his fingers brings me closer and closer until I feel like I can't take anymore.

"Don't fight it," he encouraged, and at his words, I let go, allowing the trembling to overtake my body. I clenched my eyes shut as waves of pleasure crash into me. My breath came out in a huff as I realize I'd forgotten to breath. As I came down from my high, Enzo pulled his fingers out and replaced them with the heat of his cock. I snapped my eyes open, and that cocky grin was back on his face.

"It'll fit," he said, as if reading my thoughts.

I widened my thighs as he slowly sunk into me. Inch by inch, my body started to accommodate his size. I bit down on my lip once he was fully seated inside me.

"Are you okay?" he asked.

I nodded my head, and he started to move. His hands were next to my head, keeping his weight off as he moved inside of me. Each time he did, his pelvis hit my clit, causing that familiar tingling sensation all over again. He started to move faster, and my body clenched around him as another orgasm hit me.

"Fuck!" he moaned as he emptied himself inside me.

Chapter Eight

The dull vibrating of my phone made my eyes snap open. My arms were wrapped tight around Raven, and her ass was pressed against my dick. The brightness of the phone lit up the dark bedroom. I rolled over and looked at the caller ID. It was my real estate agent. I slowly got out of the bed, careful not to wake her. We'd only just fallen asleep, and the sun wasn't even up yet. Once I closed the bedroom door, I answered the phone. "What's up?"

"Mr. Genovese, the fire department has notified me that one of the houses has caught fire. I am heading over there now. I don't know what kind of state it's in."

"Shit!" I ran a hand through my hair. Depending on how bad the damage was, restoring it would be nearly impossible. "I'm on my way."

I hung up the phone and crept back into the bedroom to grab a pair of jeans and a T-shirt. Raven's red hair was spread out over the pillow. Her face was relaxed as she snored quietly. She must have taken her dress off during the night because she was completely naked. The covers hid her breast from my view. I thought about pulling the cover down an inch just so I could see, but that would wake her, and I wanted her to be here when I came back. I crept out of the room and walked out of the apartment to the car in the garage. It was close to six a.m., so I hoped traffic wouldn't be too bad.

*****

I pulled up to the house behind the fire truck. The neighbors were outside, dressed in their pajamas, as the firefighters put out the last bit of the flames. The house was just a structure of half-standing walls. I spotted Tom standing on the sidewalk with his arms across his chest. He was dressed in a suit despite the time of day. I got out of the car and walked up to him.

"I'm sorry, Enzo," Tom said.

I gave him a grimace. "It's alright. This is part of the risk."

One of the firefighters took off his helmet and walked toward the two of us. "Mr. Genovese?"

"That's me."

"We put out the last of the flames, but as you can see, it was a pretty bad fire. It will take us a day or so to confirm but from what I can tell...this was no accident."

I looked around. Most of the people were going back to their homes to go back to sleep, but there was one group of familiar guys standing a safe distance away, arms crossed over their chests like before. I'd hoped they wouldn't cause trouble, but now, I was going to have to take action. It was a stupid mistake on their part to come after a Cosa Nostra capo.

"Arson?" Tom asked.

"We can't confirm yet, not until some of the smoke clears and we can get a good look. Is the property covered?"

I raised an eyebrow at Tom.

Tom nodded quickly. "Yes, all of the homes are covered by insurance."

"You might want to give them a call. We will notify you when you can come back on the property."

I shook the firefighter's hand. "Thank you."

Once he walked away, I turned to Tom.

"Let the insurance company know and tell me what they say. Once that's cleared up, we're going to have to tear the rest of the structure down and start anew."

Tom pulled out his phone and got to work while I walked back to my car. I had to let Giovanni, the underboss of Cosa Nostra, know about our new problem. I needed the go-ahead from him before I could put these fools in their places.

I drove along the circular driveway of Giovanni's mansion. I'd called ahead of time to see if there was a good place we could meet. Gio never slept, so I wasn't worried about that. Usually, Gio would be at the club, but rumors have been surfacing about the new woman in his life. I wondered if that was the reason Gio was still at home. I climbed the porch steps and knocked on the door. Gio's housekeeper answered. At one point, I found her to be gorgeous, with long dark hair and bright blue eyes. Her body was small and tight, the kind woman get from spending a couple of days a week at the gym, but compared to the redhead that was waiting in my bed, I barely gave Justine a second glance.

"Gio here?" I asked, already knowing the answer.

Justine nodded. "In the dining room."

I walked through the giant mansion. The place was a fortress, built for a king. Giovanni was seated at the dining room table with a plate of food in front of him. He wore a black T-shirt and sweatpants, as if just coming from the gym.

"Boss," I greeted him as I took a seat.

Giovanni put his fork down and leaned forward on the table. "What's up, Enzo?"

He could be a downright terrifying man, with eyes dark as night and a quickness to kill those who disrespected him, but he was a good, fair boss. He let the capos have freedom over our crew and territories, only stepping in if there were major problems.

"I bought some homes over on Eighth Street. Been trying to fix them up, but you know the neighborhood over there..."

A smile stretched across Gio's face. "Like hell I do. Running into problems, aren't you?"

I let out a breath. "Yeah, one of my houses burned down this morning and not by accident."

Gio chuckled and leaned back in the chair. "So what do you want to do about it?"

"Take out the leader. Get this shit over with in one swoop so it doesn't become a continuous problem."

A gang like this could continue to cause problems for us down the road, and I didn't have time to deal with it. When leaders die, organizations re-evaluated what they were doing.

Giovanni stayed silent, as if thinking it over. "How big is the gang?"

"Small. Nothing compared to my crew."

"Alright, but it's a good idea to keep tabs on them, even once the leader is taken out. I don't want this coming back to haunt us down the road. If they are just street thugs, it shouldn't be a problem."

I nodded. "Thanks, Boss."

I stood up to leave, but Giovanni put a hand up to stop me. I slid back into the seat, even though I was eager to get back home and go another round with the beautiful redhead in my bed. I should be more focused on one of my homes burning down, but Raven was stuck in my head.

"How's the gambling?" Gio asked.

"Good. Overhead is low so everything we make now is profit. People don't win very often when they have an addiction. And when they do win, they just bring it right back to lose the next night."

"Guns, coke? Everything selling?"

I nodded. "Both are selling great. I'll probably need to actually get more coke from Tommy soon. We're running low."

"Alright, let me know if you need anything else."

I got up from the chair and left. I drove at least twenty over the speed limit in anticipation of getting back to Raven. The sun was high in the sky. I wondered what time she normally woke up. If she was at the brothel until the wee hours of the morning, then she was probably still fast asleep. I took the elevator up to my floor and walked inside the apartment. I shut the door quietly behind me, but when I got to the bedroom, the bed was empty. The covers and sheets were still wrinkled and twisted together. Her shoes were missing from the floor where she'd kicked them off, and in her place sat Bello with a smile on his face and his tongue sticking out.

Chapter Nine

<u>Raven</u>

"Why are you here so early?" Erica asked with a hand on her hip while I poured myself a cup of coffee. I should be at home getting some sleep, but I didn't feel very tired. After sex, I slept like a rock for a few hours—until I heard the front door close and I realized I needed to leave. I couldn't afford to get comfortable. It was only a matter of time before I'd steal his money and I'd never see him again. Plus, I didn't want to stick around for him to throw me out. I had more decency than that.

"Dr. Eric is coming by," I said, offering a lame excuse.

Erica squinted her eyes. "So? He comes by every week to give us our STI tests. Why do you..." She trailed off and her eyes lit up as understanding hit her. "You had sex with him!"

"Shhh."

"And you didn't use a condom?" Erica shook her head, but a smile stretched across her face. "You dirty dog."

I leaned against the counter, cradling the warm coffee in my hands. "It was just one night."

Erica jumped up to sit her butt on the counter across from me. "So tell me. Was it good?"

Heat surged up to my cheeks, and I felt like I was in high school again. So stupid.

"Yes, it was good," I admitted.

"Then what's the problem?"

"I'm stealing $30,000 from him. Remember?"

Erica shrugged. "You have to steal the money anyways, so why not have fun with it?"

I looked into my caramel-colored coffee. That would be easy if I didn't feel anything, but last night wasn't just sex. I liked it too much. I couldn't get used to the feeling of someone being there for me, because when he left, I'd be the one who was hurt. He would take a piece of my heart with him when all this was over. So I had to stay away, take my money, and never see him again.

I didn't get a chance to answer Erica because a knock at the door interrupted us. Erica jumped down from the counter. "I'll get it."

I took a sip of my coffee, letting the warm liquid heat my throat. Heavy footsteps too loud to belong to one of the girls continued down the hall until Enzo was standing in the doorway of the kitchen. "Hey, baby."

My breath caught in my throat as I got a good look at him. He was dressed in a pair of dark jeans and a tight shirt that stretch across his muscular chest, a chest I had laid my head on last night until I'd fallen asleep.

"You left my apartment pretty fast this morning," he said with accusation in his eyes.

"I needed to get back to work."

He looked behind him, as if searching for customers, before taking a step inside.

"Wait," I said, stopping him in his tracks. "We shouldn't..."

"Why not?" he asked. What could I tell him? That I was planning to take money from him and didn't want to get hurt at the end? That I was scared he'd kill me once he found out what I'd done? Instead, I just stared at him like a deer caught in the headlights. He smiled at me and continued toward me. I set the coffee down on the counter behind me. His scent reminded me of his soft bed that I'd woken up in.

"I'm not done with you yet."

His words were like a direct line to my pussy, and I was powerless against Enzo's advances. I wanted this just as much as he did, but I was terrified of the inevitable fall that was just on the other side of this little affair.

I didn't fight him or offer another excuse as to why he needed to leave because I wanted him. It was reckless and stupid, but when had I ever been anything but reckless?

I hoped up on the counter and opened my legs. I wore nothing under the sundress I had on. Enzo stepped between my legs and grabbed a fistful of my hair. I gasped as he pulled my head back and sucked on my neck. It was going to leave a mark, but I didn't care. If Enzo wanted to claim me, I'd let him. My hand moved to his pants, and I quickly pulled him out. His cock fell heavy into my hand. He replaced my hand with his and I gripped the counter as I watched him plunged into me. As he pounded into me, his thrusts weren't gentle like the night before. It was like he was punishing me for leaving this morning. My body responded to his roughness as every part of me grew hot. One of his hands gripped my hair while the other grabbed one of my boobs through the thin material of my dress. He didn't play with my clit or tease me. This was all for him, and I was more than willing to give him everything he needed. I grabbed onto his ass encouraging him to keep up the pace.

"Fuck!" he groaned before his body shuddered and his muscles relaxed under my touch. He didn't give me time for my heart rate to slow. Instead, he pulled out, causing cum to drip out of me and onto the kitchen floor. He pulled up his pants, gave me a quick kiss, and walked out the door, leaving me shocked and frustrated.

*****

After taking a quick shower upstairs in the bathroom, I got checked out by Dr. Eric and stopped into Erica's room. She was pulling her hair up in a loose bun, probably getting ready to go to sleep for the day. She smirked at me as I walked in and sat on the end of her bed.

"Don't look at me like that," I warned her.

"Like what? Like you just got fucked in the kitchen by that hottie?" She walked over to the bed and sat crossed legged on the mattress.

"It's nothing."

"Whatever helps you sleep at night. Are you clean?"

"I hope so. I'll find out for sure in a couple days. That was so stupid of me."

"It happens."

"What about you?" I asked. There was a strict rule that the men had to wear condoms, but I knew some of the girls let them take it off if they paid extra, hence why I had Dr. Eric come in every week to get them tested.

"I'm sure I'm fine. I don't care how much money they offer, it's not worth getting sick. I'm trying to get my son back."

Erica had a three-year-old son that her parents currently had custody of. Like me, she'd grown up in foster care, but she'd gotten addicted to some bad stuff. From the stories Erica had told me, she went through a lot of hard times trying to stay clean. When Erica had her son, they found drugs in her system and custody was given to her parents. She'd been clean ever since the incident, but finding a job was hard with a criminal record.

"How's he doing?" I asked.

"He's good. He looks just like me." She grabbed her phone off the bedside table and pulled up a picture to show me a curly-haired little boy with a grin spread across his face.

"He's adorable," I said, my chest filling with joy. I wondered what it would be like to have a little mini-me running around.

"Thanks. I miss him, but he's better with my parents—at least until I can get an apartment and find a real job to show the court."

I could see the love and longing in Erica's eyes. She visited her son every weekend and stayed sober for him. I was reminded again as to what would happen if I didn't get the money I needed to the Irish. I had to do it...for Erica.

I stood up from the bed. "I should let you get some sleep."

"I'll see you tonight?"

"Yeah, I'll be a little late again. I'm going back to the underground."

Chapter Ten

"Hey, baby," I said into the phone as I exited the black SUV. Dave, my enforcer, drove me today. It was always smart to have an extra pair of hands during tribute.

"Why is there a man outside my business like some kind of bodyguard?" Raven spat.

"Well, did you ask him why he was there?" A grin tugged at my lips as I walked through the front door of the house with Dave following behind me. The house was located on the outskirts of the Bronx, so I wasn't too worried about being targeted.

"Yeah, and he said you told him to be here, and if I had a problem, I could take it up with you."

The only furniture in the house was a large oak dining room table that my men were sitting around, chatting quietly, as they waited for me. Instead of going immediately to the table, I walked up the stairs to the second floor to continue my conversation.

"Well, I guess you have your answer, don't you?"

"Enzo, I don't need some scary-looking man standing outside my business. He's going to scare away customers."

I scoffed. "I doubt that." My man standing outside wasn't going to deter anyone from getting some pussy, but it would make them think twice before doing something stupid.

"Enzo..." she warned.

"Baby..." She didn't say anything for a minute. "Why are you always so quick to prove that you can do things yourself?" I asked her.

She needed someone there for protection. That was obvious the first time I went to the brothel. But what I didn't understand is why she wouldn't accept the help when I was giving it to her on a silver platter.

"Do you always do this for your one-night stands?" She asked, avoiding my question.

"No. Just you."

She huffed. Obviously, she was used to getting her way. "Make him leave," she demanded.

"Not a chance, baby. I'm going into a meeting. I'll see you tonight."

I hung up before she could respond and went back downstairs. The hardwood creaked under my feet as I walked. The house was still under construction, which meant the floors had been sawed and buffed and were ready to be stained a deep cherry wood.

"Boss," Leon greeted as I came around the corner to take my seat at the head of the table. I didn't acknowledge him. I was still slightly pissed from having to break up the fight between him and Charles a few weeks ago.

Each man had either a duffle bag or book bag at their feet containing my cut of their money. My crew was more senior than most. Almost all of them were made men, which meant they knew what they were doing so I could focus on other aspects of the business.

"How's it goin', Boss?" Cole asked from my right side.

"Just livin' the life. I heard you had a good month," I said. Cole looked uncomfortable in the chair he was sitting in. He was six-foot-five and at least 230 pounds. He'd come on as an enforcer until we realized he was a mean motherfucker with a sniper. Now, he did any hit jobs that we needed.

"Yeah, not bad."

I nodded. "Good to hear."

I looked around the table to see that the men had gone quiet as they waited for me to speak.

"Pass them up and I'll listen to any updates," I said, waving the men forward. One by one, they got up and dropped their bags off at my feet. Once everyone was done and back in their chairs, I picked up one of the bags, took out a stack of rubber-banded bills, and started counting. Dave took a bag and started counting as well. Everyone stayed quiet until I nodded at Leon.

"What's going on, Leon?" I asked, my eyes focused on the money.

"We have a couple deals coming through next week for AKs. I'm running a little low, but shipment is supposed to be coming in soon."

"Rizzo, everything on track with the shipment? If we said we were going to come through on this deal, I don't want to mess it up," I said, looking up for just a moment to flash my eyes to the skinny guy at the end of the table.

"Everything's good on my end."

I rubber-banded the cash together and wrote the amount down on the notebook next to me before grabbing a second stack to start counting.

I nodded at Cole.

"Nothing new on my end. Of course, I'd let you know if I run into any problems."

I nodded to let him know I'd heard him. We went around the table like that, each man filling me in on any news or updates while Dave and I counted the money. No one left until every dollar was counted for.

A percentage of my money got kicked up to Giovanni, who then kicked some up to Cassandra. That's how the chain went, and the higher up you were, the more money you got to keep. I cleared my throat, causing my men to quiet down.

"Just one more thing before you go on your way. We have a problem with one of the street gangs."

"You talkin' about the one on Eighth Street?" Chris, a small guy covered in tattoos, asked.

"Yeah, we're going to take out their leader, so stay clear of them for a little while. We don't need any hostility in the streets. Hopefully once we take him out, that will be the end of it."

I looked around the table, and everyone nodded in understanding.

"Cole, you need some sniping practice?" I asked.

Cole smiled at me. "Always, Boss."

"We'll meet to figure out the details. Everyone's good to go."

I waved them on, and the chairs scratched against the floors as they got up to leave.

*****

It was barely dark outside when I pulled up to the brothel. I could see the lights were on but didn't know if Raven would be here. Gunner stood outside the door in a dark suit. His broad shoulders and cold stare made him a scary sight. I doubted anybody would try anything with Gunner standing right outside.

"Boss," Gunner greeted.

"She inside?" I asked.

"Just got here a few minutes ago."

"Perfect."

I walked inside and spotted her sitting behind the front desk. She was bent over as if ruffling with something below the desk. Her head popped up when the door shut behind me.

"I was just getting ready to leave. Had to stop by to grab something." She stuffed something in her jeans, and the safe clicked closed.

"Where you going?" I asked, taking a step closer and leaning against the desk.

"To the underground."

My eyes flickered to the clock on the wall. "A little early, isn't it?"

She shrugged. "I have something to take care of here tonight."

"How about we go out for some food first?" I phrased it like a question to try not to piss her off, but I already had a reservation at a nice restaurant a couple blocks north from here. She looked down at her outfit, jeans and a low-cut blouse.

"I don't know if I'm..."

"You look beautiful," I said. The words were out of my mouth before I could stop them, but they were true. No matter what she was wearing, she was still the most beautiful thing I'd laid eyes on. She pulled her bottom lip into her mouth as if debating my offer.

"Come on, baby. It's just dinner."

She rolled her eyes. "Fine." She stood up and rounded the desk to join me in front.

"Where are all the girls at?" I asked, looking around the empty foyer.

"Either getting ready or with a client already," she said as we walked out the door and down the stairs.

"Does it ever bother you?" I asked once we got in the car.

"Does what bother me?"

"Being in the business. Just knowing that those girls are selling themselves?" I had no room to judge. God knows I was in some of the shadiest businesses, but I had grown up in it and I was a man.

"Not at all. My girls don't do drugs or get in trouble. A lot of them came from not the greatest backgrounds. They're just doing what they have to do. There was a point in my life where I could have easily followed that same path."

My eyes flickered to her. She was facing away from me, toward the window. I wanted to ask more questions, but I didn't want to push. Raven had a story behind those beautiful eyes.

I parked the car and went around to open Raven's door, but she hadn't waited for me and was already standing on the sidewalk.

"Let me open the door for you."

She crossed her arms over her chest. "Why?"

"Because that's how you should be treated. If you're going out with me, you shouldn't have to lift a finger, so you can leave your 'I can do it' attitude at home."

"I'm not helpless. I don't need someone to open my doors and watch over my business."

"It's not about needing it. You don't have to keep proving that you are capable of doing things on your own. We all know you can. Now come on." This woman was going to drive me crazy. I tugged lightly on her elbow until she uncrossed her arms and followed me inside.

"Enzo?" The hostess asked as I walked up the stand.

"Yes."

"Right this way."

She led us past all the tables and to a set of stairs. I kept my hand on Raven's lower back as we climbed the stairs to the rooftop. Only ten or so table were up here, and three of them were occupied. The hostess sat us at the table furthest away from everyone else.

"Thank you," I told the her before slipping a one-hundred-dollar bill in her hand. She blushed before turning away and going back down the stairs.

Raven looked out over the city, her eyes wide.

"Beautiful, isn't it?" I asked. From where we sat, we could see the entire city lit up with lights.

"This...it's amazing."

A smile spread across my face. I'd never taken a woman out on a date. I never needed to. Not when they were all too willing to let me take them home, but Raven was different. I hadn't even thought about another girl since I'd walked her home that night. I was completely out of my element here, but I was glad it sounded like I'd done something right.

"Can I get you two something to drink?" The waiter asked, appearing next to the table. I ordered a bottle of wine and then focused my attention back to Raven. Her hair was down tonight, and it fluttered in the wind. It fell down her back in long waves. Her face was free of any makeup, but she was still more beautiful than any other woman I've ever set my eyes on. I kept my eyes on her plump lips as she brought her glass of water to them. I imagined those lips wrapped tightly around my cock.

I cleared my throat, trying to cover up the fact that I'd been eye-fucking her. "You live far away?"

"No. I like to keep close to the business in case anything happens."

She reminded me of a lotus flower, growing from the mud and dirt into the strong beautiful woman across from me.

"What about you? Parents?" she asked.

I nodded. "Yeah, my mom lives in Manhattan with my younger sister. Dad passed away several years back."

"I'm sorry."

"Thank you."

The waiter came back and poured us our wine.

"So, your dad, was he..." she trailed off once the waiter left with our orders.

"He was involved. He was taken out by a rival...it happens."

It was a risk you take when you were a part of Cosa Nostra. There were going to be enemies no matter how careful you were. I was usually more private about my work, but she owned a brothel, so it wasn't like she could rat on me.

"My mom wants me to stop working so much. I think she worries that I'll end up like my father or miss out on a lot of life," I continued.

"Well, are you? Missing out on life?" she asked, taking a sip of her wine.

"I enter alive and I will have to get out dead." It's the exact words every man speaks to become made. There was no way out.

"Don't you get tired of it? Always being on the go from one place to another? Where'd you go when I spent the night?"

It was the same questions my mom asked. I knew my body was tired, and I wasn't sleeping nearly enough. It was like I was on a constant high. Sometimes I felt almost manic, but like a junkie, I got off on the adrenaline. Nothing good came from being a sitting duck.

"Tired or not, it's what I signed up for."

She didn't look at me in admiration for my accomplishments like most women did. She wasn't impressed by my nice watch or suit. Instead, when I looked into her soft blue eyes, I saw pity looking back.

"What do you do outside of work? How many businesses do you own?"

"A lot. It doesn't leave room for much else."

The waiter came back with our food.

"What about you? What do you do outside of being a pimp?" I asked.

Her lips twisted into a smile. "I'm not a pimp...or a madam. I just make sure my girls are taken care of."

I heard the sincerity in her voice. She really felt like she was taking care of those girls. It was as if she didn't realize these women were the same age as her.

We both focused on eating our food. She asked me more about Bello and how I came to own the dog. By the time we finished, I hadn't realized that the people at the surrounding tables had left.

"We should probably go," she said, noticing the empty rooftop.

We left the restaurant and went back to my car. She didn't say anything as I headed toward my place. All night, I had watched her lips as she sipped her wine, and I had the dirtiest thoughts running through my head.

I never slept with a woman more than once, and now, I was bringing her back to my place for a third go-around. I hadn't even so much as looked at another woman since talking with Raven. As soon as we walked in the door, my hands were on her. I latched my arms behind her knees and lifted her up so I could carry her to the couch. My lips never left hers as I set her down on the couch and hovered above her. She moaned quietly against my mouth as I reached under her shirt, feeling the softness of her smooth skin underneath. She pulled away long enough to lift her shirt over her head, and I took the time to remove all my clothes. Her blue eyes were glazed over with lust. She looked like such an innocent woman, but she was the most dangerous creature I had come in contact with. She had a power over me that I didn't want to acknowledge. She spread her legs, inviting me in. I hooked a finger in the waist band of her panties and took them off, leaving them in a pile on the floor.

"Fuck!" she moaned as I buried himself inside her.

Chapter Eleven

The sunlight streaming through the curtains shone on my face. I cracked open one eye, expecting Enzo to be next to me. But, just like the day before, the bed was empty. That man didn't sit still for long. I sat up in bed, clutching the covers close to my body. I was still completely naked, and my thighs were coated with the stickiness from our mixed arousal from last night. My phone on the bedside table lit up with a text message. I grabbed it to see that there were several, all from Erica. Shit, I'd told her I was going to come back last night. She was probably having a mini heart attack thinking something happened to me. I sent her a quick text letting her know I was safe before looking around the room. My clothes were laying on the bedroom floor where I'd left them last night. I took a moment to listen, to see if there was any movement on the other side of the door. Once satisfied, I climbed out of the bed, leaving the covers behind to get in the shower. His en suite bathroom was just as big and luxurious as the rest of the apartment. The shower and bathtub were separate. I imagined myself soaking in the big tub until my skin was pruney. It was doubtful that Enzo got much use out of the bathtub anyways. Shaking my head, I turned to the shower. His body wash sat on one of the shelves. The smell of citrus and leather filled the shower as I rubbed it over my skin. Once finished, I wrapped a big brown towel around my body and walked out of the bedroom. At the same time, the front door opened and Enzo walked inside with Bello. He was already fully dressed in a pair of jeans and a black T-shirt that outlined his tight biceps. His short hair curled at the top like usual, and his sharp jawline looked more prominent, like he'd just shaved. He cocked an eyebrow at me before grinning.

"I used your shower. I hope that's alright," I said, clutching the towel a little closer to me.

"You can do whatever you want, baby," he said, before unhooking Bello and hanging his leash back up. The dog immediately ran over to me. I prepared myself for him to jump on me, but instead, he stuck his tongue out and licked a droplet of water running off my leg. I laughed and bent down to pet the big love bug. Enzo grabbed a bag of dog food from a cabinet and poured it into the large dog bowl. Bello walked away from me and went to eat. I followed the dog into the kitchen area and opened the fridge. There wasn't much inside, but I grabbed a cartoon of eggs and some veggies and set them on the counter.

"Are you going somewhere?" I asked Enzo, realizing I'd assumed I could stay for breakfast. Maybe I was being presumptuous. More than most people, I knew that sex didn't have to go further than the bedroom. But, from the way he'd come charging after me when I left last time, I thought it was better to stay at least for a little while.

He shook his head. "Not anymore."

He grabbed me around the waist and pulled me against his body. My skin instantly started to heat up from our close contact. He smelled just like the body wash I used this morning.

"Are you cooking for me?" he asked, his voice tickling my ear as he spoke into it. How could I already be so turned on when we just had sex?

I raised an eyebrow in fake surprise. "Oh, did you want some?"

He slapped my ass, then released me to sit on the wooden stool at the butcher-block top island. I could feel his eyes on me as I heated up the pan and whisked the eggs together in a bowl.

"Who taught you to cook?" he asked.

"No one. I'm not great at it, but I can make scrambled eggs and toast."

"That's more than I can do," he admitted. That wasn't surprising. Most New Yorkers relied heavily on take-out. I'd only learned how to cook out of necessity. When money was tight, it was a lot cheaper to cook at home.

I finished breakfast and plated the food. Enzo's phone vibrated against the counter as I set the plate down in front of him.

"Do you need to get that?" I asked when he didn't immediately pick it up.

"I'm busy. Whatever it is, it can wait."

I couldn't help but be a little shocked. I'm sure Enzo dealt with a lot of issues that could be life or death and ignoring his phone was probably something he didn't do often. I sat down across from him and started to eat.

We ate in comfortable silence as Bello laid at my feet, probably hoping for a piece of food to be dropped on the ground. A knock sounded at the door. Enzo didn't look surprised. He got up from the stool and disappeared to answer the door.

"Boss," a deep voice said. Boss? How far up was Enzo on the food chain? He said he owned the Bronx, but I assumed he was just being cocky. I heard hands slapping together before I got up to take my plate to the sink. Enzo cleared his throat. I turned to see him standing beside a huge man. He towered over Enzo, both in height and muscle, which was saying a lot since Enzo was a big man himself.

"Raven, this is Cole. Cole, Raven."

I tightened the towel around my body. Damn, I should have put some clothes on.

"Hello," I greeted.

Cole nodded at me.

"I'll be right back. Don't go anywhere," Enzo commanded.

His demeanor changed from the person I'd been eating breakfast with a moment ago to something much...darker. This was the facade he must put on in front of other men. Men that couldn't see him as weak. I nodded, and they walked down the hall to what must have been a back room. Not sure what else to do. I washed the few dishes I'd used and went back to Enzo's bedroom to put on my clothes from last night. As I slid them over my body, I heard the men talking. They must have been in the room next door.

"The firefighter confirmed arson, so we are good to go forward with the hit," Enzo said.

"I will need to track him for a few days to find out his routine before I can take him out." They were talking about killing someone. I shouldn't have been surprised. I knew what Enzo did for a living, but it didn't match the man that had taken me out for dinner last night. He was like two different people living in the same body.

"That's fine. I'm not in a big hurry."

The sound of glass clinked as if he was pouring a drink, even though it was still early in the day.

"So who's the girl?" Cole asked. I held my breath, waiting for Enzo's response.

"Just a one-night thing."

My heart sank at his words, and I couldn't figure out why. I figured Enzo was probably a guy who took a new girl home every night. Why was I feeling such disappointment? I buttoned my pants and pulled on my shirt. I slung my purse over my shoulder and walked out of the apartment.

Chapter Twelve

The door slammed shut, and I closed my eyes in irritation. Raven couldn't listen if her life depended on it.

"Sounds like your one-night thing just left," Cole said.

"You still have that hacker guy?" I asked him. I didn't want Cole to know that Raven was more than a one-night stand, especially when I wasn't entirely sure what we were doing. Raven would have a target on her back for associating with me, and I didn't want that to happen unless we were a sure thing. She still didn't trust me; her guard went up the moment we stopped fucking.

"I need you to have him look into someone for me." I grabbed a piece of paper off my desk and wrote down Raven's name and passed it to him. "Let me know what you find out."

Cole nodded. "Anything else?"

"No, just check in with me once you've had your eyes on Dominic for a few days."

Cole nodded and got up from the chair. I walked him out and then turned around to look at the empty apartment. I was rarely here if I wasn't sleeping, and the short moment of quietness was starting to get to me. Raven must have cleaned up the kitchen while I was talking with Cole because it was back to its original state as if she'd never been there. I grabbed my keys off the hook and headed out the door.

*****

"She's not here," said Erica. She'd introduced herself last time I was here. She looked more like she belonged at a Coachella concert with the long flowy dress she wore. Black hair fell across her shoulders. None of the girls I'd seen at the brothel looked like typical prostitutes. Raven could easily raise the prices and make this into a high-end place.

"Where is she?" I asked. Dave stood outside when I'd approached the building. I had two men keeping watch over the brothel and they switched out from time to time.

"Maybe I should be asking you that, since she didn't come here last night," she said with a hand on her hip.

"Where's her apartment?"

She looked taken back by my question.

"You can either tell me, or I'll figure it out on my own. I'm not stalking her."

Erica narrowed her eyes at me as if debating if she should give out Raven's address. After a moment, she sighed and walked around the desk to pick up a piece of paper. She wrote something down and handed it to me. "When you find her, tell her to call the brothel so I know she's alive. That text she sent was not enough to prove life."

I pulled a wad of cash from my pocket and set it on the desk. "Thanks for the help."

I walked away before she could protest. I exchanged a handshake with Dave before looking at the piece of paper in my hand. She lived close enough that driving would be a waste of time. The street was still pretty busy with people going to work. My phone vibrated in my pocket, but I ignored it for now. The phone never stopped ringing. I'd deal with whatever it was once I was done at Raven's. I was tired of her running off.

*****

Her apartment wasn't as nice as I'd imagined. The brothel had to be bringing in a decent amount of money. Prostitutes weren't cheap, but from Raven's apartment, you couldn't tell. It wasn't bad. The brick exterior of the building looked clean, but there wasn't any kind of security at the door. I didn't have to put in a security code or be buzzed in. She should be in an apartment with at least a door code.

The front door opened up to a tile hallway. It was quiet in the building, probably because everyone was at work. My steps echoed as I walked the hall, looking for her apartment number. She was on the second floor at the very end. I knocked and stuffed my hands in my pockets. After a moment, I knocked again, this time louder. No response.

"We both know I can get in this apartment if I want to, baby," I said loud enough that she would hear through the door. Another minute passed. *Guess I'm going to have to break in.* The sound of a chain clinking filled the hallway before she opened the door. Her hair was still wet from the shower she'd taken at my house. She'd changed into a pair of cotton shorts that showed off her long slender legs and a tight T-shirt that stretched across her tits.

"What do you want?" she snapped, looking annoyed.

"Why the sass?" I asked, confused by her sudden change in attitude. This morning, I thought we were fine. Did I fucking miss something?

She didn't answer. Instead, she leaned against the door frame and waited.

"Why'd you leave? I told you to stay."

"Why do you care? I'm just a one-night thing anyways, right?"

My eyebrows furrowed together as I tried to figure out what she was talking about. It's been a long time since I've tried to solve one of these stupid riddles that women dish out instead of just coming right out with it. Then it hit me. She must have heard when I was talking to Cole.

"Raven—"

"Just go, Enzo. I have things to do."

She slammed the door in my face before I could even defend myself. It would be easy to pick the lock and let myself in, but that would only piss her off more. I ground my molars together. Why the fuck had she been listening to our conversation? I should just let it go. It was stupid for me to keep sleeping with her anyway. It's not like I could actually offer her anything besides money. I couldn't be someone's husband who was home every night for dinner. That just wasn't the reality of the world I lived in. My phone vibrated again. I pulled it out and answered.

"There's something you need to see, here at the underground," Gunner said. I looked at the Raven's apartment door one more time before letting out a sigh.

"I'll be right there."

Walking into the underground was like going from day to night. There was no sense of time down here. That's probably why people stayed so long, not even realizing the whole day had passed them by. It wasn't busy at this time. Despite their gambling problems, most of the men had day jobs they were trying desperately to maintain, even if it was just so they made enough to come back here each night. I looked around for

Gunner but didn't see him anywhere on the floor. I passed the tables and bar, heading toward the back room. I never spent much time in here. It was a small space with only a couple chairs and a wall full of monitors showing everything happening on the gambling floor. Gunner was seated in the chair, dressed in a suit. He looked uncomfortable in the small chair. He was a big motherfucker with dark, cold eyes. He'd been an enforcer for Cosa Nostra for a long-ass time and had killed more people than I can count.

"What's going on?" I asked before closing the door and taking the empty office chair next to him.

"You aren't going to like this," he said, giving him a hard look.

"Just show me. I have to go by the club to pick up some blow from Tommy in a few."

Gunner turned back to the screens and typed a few things on the keyboard until they all showed the same camera. It was dated a few weeks ago. He pressed play and sat back in the chair.

I watched the screen for a while. It was a busy night, and almost all the tables were filled. I spotted myself at the bar.

"What the fuck am I looking at?" I asked.

"Your girl."

It only took a minute to spot her at the blackjack table. Gunner pressed a few buttons on the keyboard to zoom in on her. She was dressed in a tight black dress that gave me the perfect view of her cleavage. I watched for a few minutes as she played, thought I didn't see anything out of ordinary. I was about to tell Gunner to stop wasting my time when I noticed her hand. It moved from the top of the table to underneath. I leaned closer to the screen. Her fingers were moving. She was counting on her fingers like a child would do. Her eyes scanned the cards in front of her opponents as she continued to count.

"She's counting," I said.

Gunner nodded. "She's gotten a lot better since that night. I think she was practicing."

I ground my teeth together, trying to stay in control of my anger.

She played me. She's been playing me like a fool.

"Then why hasn't she won anything?" I gritted out as my fists clenched until my knuckles turned white.

Gunner shrugged. "Maybe she's saving up for a big win?"

Why would she need a big win? She had an entire brothel at her fingertips. Something wasn't adding up, but either way, she had me right where she wanted me. I'd underestimated her. It was stupid of me not to ask more questions. Air came hissing through my nose like an angry bull.

I had to take care of this before it got out of hand. If I let her get away with stealing from me, I'd look weak. I'd lose all the respect I spent years building. I wasn't as harsh as some of the men, like Giovanni, but when you were in the mob, there were things you had to do to keep your respect, whether you liked it or not. If she was a man, I wouldn't bat an eyelash at killing him. I'd hunt him down right now. But I'd stupidly let her crawl into my bed. And damn was she good in bed.

"What are you going to do, Boss?" Gunner asked.

Chapter Thirteen

"I'm doing it tonight," I said to Erica as I walked into her bedroom. Erica sat on the bed with a mirror perched on her knees as she applied her makeup.

She looked up with wide eyes. "Why tonight? He came here looking for you."

Because I needed to protect myself. Because Enzo made it clear that I'm just a booty call and I can't let myself get wrapped up. I crossed the room and sat on the edge of the bed. I'd chosen to wear a pair of tight skinny jeans and a loose top. Hopefully, I won't draw too much attention to myself.

"I just need to do it, get it over with, pay off the Irish, and go back to living my life. A life without Enzo or the Irish."

"You really think he's going to let you go that easy?"

Yes, because he didn't really care to begin with. He wanted me for sex, and he got what he wanted. He was just like every other man, just like the Johns that came in here at night, except Enzo didn't have to pay for sex. I'd given it out for free.

"What choice do I have? I can't sit around expecting someone to save me. You know as well as I do. That never happens. Women like us don't get saved by Prince Charming. We have to do it ourselves."

Erica stared at me for a moment, processing everything I'd said.

"What do you need from me?" she asked finally.

"Just take care of things here. I'm going to disappear for a week or so. If everything is fine, I'll come back."

Now that Enzo somehow knew where I lived, I couldn't hide out there anymore. Luckily, there was an empty apartment above Toby's bar that he said I could stay in.

"And if everything is not fine? If he comes looking for you, then what?"

"I don't know."

There wasn't much time to think about the potential consequences. Either Enzo or the Irish would come knocking at my door again soon if I didn't hurry up and do this.

Erica stood up from the bed, letting the small mirror fall to the side. She crouched down to look under the bed and tossed me a pair of bright red heels.

"Here. If you're going to risk everything...at least do it in heels."

I changed from my sneakers into the heels. When I stood up, Erica engulfed me in a hug.

"Be careful, Raven. I know you act like you're doing this for your own pride and independence, but I know you're doing it to keep us safe. That's a helluva lot more than anyone has ever done for me."

I swallowed the lump in my throat and smiled at Erica. I was afraid if I talked, the tears would start to stream down my face, and I'd spend too long on my makeup to ruin it now. Erica took a step back, allowing me to walk past and out of the door.

*****

I took a deep breath and squared my shoulders before walking down the steps to the underground. Butterflies erupted in my stomach, and my heart was in my throat. This was it. I was finally doing what should have been done a week ago. Hopefully, Enzo wouldn't pay me any attention. It would be even better if he wasn't there tonight.

The man at the door smiled before holding it open. The smell of smoke and whiskey filled my nose. Glasses clinked together at the bar area, and the sound of cards being shuffled bounced off the cement walls. After this, I'd never come back to the underground. Hell, I might never come back to the Bronx or maybe even New York depending on how this panned out. I reminded myself why I was doing all this. Why I was risking my life and business as I knew it. It was for the women back at the house who'd never had anybody look after them before. I couldn't let them be taken when they'd already been through so much.

Much to my relief, the place was packed. Maybe I'd blend in easier. I crossed the room to an open spot at the blackjack table. Staying close to the door for a fast exit would have been the smart thing to do, but all the blackjack tables were near the back of the room.

"You in?" the dealer asked. He was a skinny man with a gun on hip that looked like it was weighing down his jeans.

I grabbed the wad of cash out my purse and set it in the middle of the table. I should be smart and lose a few hands before getting on my winning streak. But I also wanted to hurry this up while Enzo wasn't here. The dealer started to deal the first round of cards. It was going to take at least three games for my counting to be accurate.

My first card was a five, but the man to left of me had a face card as well as the man seated two spots away from me. The second round of cards was dealt. Only one other face card turned up. I was given a two of spades. We currently had three face cards on the table. I assigned each card a number and quickly realized I was going to lose this hand. The man to my right hit twenty-one exactly. He took his money and left the stool. I crossed my fingers, hoping someone else would show up. It was easier to count with more people playing. A man dressed in a suit took the seat beside me and added more money to the pile.

I won the second game, which was enough for me to break even. After that, I kept winning. By game six, I was halfway there with fifteen thousand in my purse. I could take it all home in this next game. The other players probably thought my luck was running out because they raised their ante. The pile of money in the middle grew. The door closed and the air shifted in the room. I didn't even have to turn around to know he'd walked in. I could feel his presence. I shifted in my seat and focused on the game. Maybe he wouldn't notice me. I can win this hand and then get out. I bounced my leg, wishing the dealer would get the cards out faster. The men around me were screwed. One had busted, three were short by at least five. The dealer pointed at me. I tapped the table, indicating I wanted another card.

I hit twenty-one. The men groaned. Some got up to leave. I quickly grabbed my money, stuffed it in my purse and made my way to the door. The walk seemed so much longer now with over thirty-thousand dollars in my bag and the feel of Enzo's eyes on me. I avoided looking his way, afraid it would make me lose my nerve. I tried to stay calm but all I wanted to do was break into a run to get to that door faster. My heart beat loud in my ears. I wasn't far from the door now. I did it. I was going to hand this money over to the Irish and take back ownership of my brothel. I'd never have to tell the girls about the real threat that had been circling over their heads. I could taste the freedom on the tip of my tongue.

That's when the bodyguard, who was usually on the other side of the door, blocked my path. His big arms crossed over his chest. Chills ran over my body as if someone had splashed me with ice cold water.

"I think you're forgetting something," Enzo's voice came from behind me. It was deep and had a darker tone than usual. Fuck. Fuck. Fuck. I squeezed my eyes shut for a moment before turning around. He was standing behind me in a three-piece suit. His jaw twitched, and he leveled me with a glare. Even in the seriousness of my situation, I couldn't deny how attracted to him I was. He was going to kill me. Everyone in the room stopped what they were doing to watch the scene unfold. Enzo's eyes flickered to my purse.

"Cal," Enzo said. A large man came from behind me and ripped the purse off my shoulder before setting it down on the nearby table.

"Hey! I won that—"

Enzo put a finger up, cutting me off mid-sentence. I'd never seen eyes so cold. In this moment, it was hard to imagine that I had been laying in his bed just this morning. I tried not to think about the man he'd killed at my brothel. He'd done it so fast, without thinking. Would he do the same to me? He walked toward the purse and dumped the entire thing upside down. All the money fell on to the table. Some of it spilled onto the floor along with my house keys and wallet. He let the purse drop out of his hand, onto the pile of money. I had the urge to wipe my sweaty palms on my jeans, but I was too afraid to move. He looked up from the pile of money to me as he took a gun out of his waistband.

"Enzo, please," I begged, my dignity flying out the window. I couldn't leave those girls in the house alone, helpless to the Irish. Tears streamed down my face.

"On your knees," he commanded. His face lacked even a hint of emotion. Like the time we'd spent together meant nothing. I should have known that from the beginning. Enzo was a mobster, and the mob would always come first. I was a fool.

"Enzo...I didn't have a choice," I cried. He ignored me and nodded at his bodyguard, who pushed me forward until I was on my knees in front of him. The barrel of the gun pressed against my skull, and I closed my eyes, hiccuping as I tried to get my tears under control. This was it. This was where my life ended up, from foster care to dying in the middle of an illegal gambling ring. I prepared myself for the inevitable.

When it doesn't come, I opened my eyes and looked up at Enzo. He still had the gun pressed against my head, but I could see something underneath his cold demeanor. A softness beneath the evil. The man I'd gotten to know the past weeks, he was still in there.

"Boss?" Cal asked from behind me. Enzo continued to stare as if wrestling with his own mind.

"I didn't have a choice. I had to save them," I pleaded. His jaw twitched again. He might really pull the trigger. He dropped his arm. I let out a breath I hadn't realized I was holding. Enzo walked over to Cal and whispered something to him. Then, my hands were tied behind my back. I was yanked to my feet and carried out of the underground.

I stayed quiet as Cal tossed me into the back of a black SUV. I landed on my shoulder, and pain shot down my arm. He slammed the door and sped off. I righted myself in the seat so that I was sitting up straight. I wasn't dead. That was the good thing. The bad thing was I had no idea where I was going or what Enzo would do to me once I was there. Maybe he just didn't want to kill me in front of so many witnesses. I thought about the money that was back at the underground, overflowing off the table. The Irish would be coming for me in a matter of days, and all my effort would be for nothing.

All the risks I took, putting my life on the line, was all for nothing because the girls were going to get taken. A single tear fell out of my eye and slid down my cheek. I wanted to stay strong, but there was no point now. I looked out the window. We were approaching a familiar area. Cal stopped outside Enzo's apartment. Why would he have me taken here? Enzo wouldn't kill me in his apartment...would he? Cal opened the door and grabbed me by the arm and yanked me out of the car. I stumbled onto the sidewalk, struggling to keep my balance with my hands tied behind me.

"Don't talk to anyone," Cal growled into my ear as he dragged me into the building. We rode the elevator up to Enzo's floor. The lobby and hallways were completely empty so I didn't have anyone to talk to anyway. He opened the apartment door and pushed me inside. I manage to catch myself against the wall. He made quick work of untying my wrists.

"Don't try to run. I'll be right on the other side of this door. The windows all have alarms on them if you're stupid enough to think you can survive a ten-story jump."

With those parting words, he slammed the door shut, leaving me alone in the apartment. I slid to the floor and wrapped my arms around my knees. I buried my face in my knees and allowed myself to sob.

I cried for Erica. She'd never be able to get custody of her son. All of my girls would be battered and abused because I couldn't pull this off. I didn't want to think about the horrors that the Irish would put them through. They'd probably sell them off on auction blocks like pigs for slaughter. I looked up at the sound of nails tapping against the floor as Bello walked into the room. He rested his head on my elbows, as if feeling my sadness. I wiped the tears from my face and walked to the couch. Bello followed and jumped up next to me. I petted the dog for a long while before my eyes drifted close.

Chapter Fourteen

"You can go," I told Cal as I walked up to my apartment door.

"You sure she's not goin' to run?" he asked.

I shook my head. "Nah, she knows we'll find her."

Cal hesitated.

"I think I can handle her," I said, trying to keep my anger in check.

He pushed off the door and went to the elevator. I took a deep breath before walking into the apartment. Light from the rising sun streamed in through the window, highlighting small dust particles in the air. I locked the door behind me and waited for Bello to greet me. After a moment of nothing, I set my keys down and walked across the room. The kitchen and dining room were quiet. I walked around the corner and spotted her snoring lightly on the living room couch. Bello slept beside her, curled up into her side. Her lips were puffy, and her face is smeared with makeup from her tears, but she still looks absolutely gorgeous. I'm beyond pissed at her. If it had been anyone else, I wouldn't have hesitated to kill her right there in front of everyone. It would have been a good reminder not to fuck with me. Now, I look weak. Weakness like that would lead to other people thinking they can steal from me. I should have killed her.

Bello's eyes popped open, as if he finally sensed my presence. He didn't wag his tail or jump up like I expected. Instead, the dog just stared at me. Even my own dog was mad at me. I walked out of the living room and back to the kitchen.

It was nearly six a.m. now. My body was exhausted, but I can't sleep. I'd spent the night wallowing in anger before coming home. I haven't used the coffee pot since I've moved into this place, but I grabbed it now and started to brew a pot. I needed to get answers, and Raven isn't going to give them to me. Plus, I didn't trust her, even if she did offer up so sort of explanation for stealing from me. I had to find out what was going on. Jacob was looking into the brothel. I needed to meet up with him soon. I leaned against the counter and watched as the coffee slowly dripped into the pot. I didn't turn around as I listened to her walk toward me. Her steps were hesitant.

"What are you going to do with me?" she asked quietly, her voice filled with sleep. It was the same question I asked myself over and over again.

"I haven't decided yet," I said, not taking my eyes off the coffee pot.

"Enzo—"

I turned to glare at her. "I don't want to hear the excuses. You stole from a high-ranking made man. Do you know the kind of torture I would have put you through if you were a man?"

She flinched as if I'd struck her. Bello, who sat beside her, let out a bark. She fidgeted with a ring on her finger as her lip quivered.

There was an empty feeling in my stomach. I hated being the one to make her cry. I wanted to wrap her in my arms and kill the person that hurt her. But that person was me, and I couldn't do anything but watch her fall apart in my kitchen while I stood there like an asshole.

I grabbed two ceramic mugs out of the cabinet.

"Sit down," I said.

She walked over to the island and sat in the metal chair. I poured both of us coffee. Remembering the way she liked her coffee, I took out a container of coffee creamer and sugar before setting it down in front of her. Her eyes were red with tears, but she lifted the side of her mouth into a sad smile as she used the spoon to start putting her coffee together.

The room was silent as we sipped our drink.

"You aren't allowed to leave this house. I'll have Cal pick up some of your stuff from the apartment. If you need something, I'll have someone go get it. I'll have a man outside the brothel at all times like I do now."

"So I'm a prisoner?" she asked.

"Be grateful that you're alive to be a prisoner," I snapped. She looked back down at the coffee.

"I didn't have a choice. I had to get thirty-thousand dollars. Everything I have is at risk," she blurted out.

I narrowed my eyes at her. I wanted her to tell me the story, but I can't believe her right now. When people get desperate, they do stupid things, so maybe there really was something big at risk.

"We'll see about that," I said. I got up from the stool, leaving my coffee cup on the island. I grabbed my keys off the small table by the door and left.

*****

"What do you got for me?" I asked Jacob, the private investigator that sat across from me at the burger joint. I owned the place. It was designed like an 80s diner. It was a hot spot during the summer, but right now, it wasn't open to the public.

"It took a lot of digging, but I think your girl is in some hot water." Jacob was in his early sixties. He'd been a cop at one point in his life until he realized he could make a lot more money playing for the other team. He spent five years in prison for it.

"Like what?"

"She grew up in foster care. Bounced from foster home to foster home. She got kicked out of a lot of them. Once she was eighteen, she started helping a local street thug get drugs across state lines for a pretty penny. She hung around some bad people, pimps, drug dealers, those types. Then she met Ben. He owned the brothel. I checked and it looks like he built the thing from the ground up, but from what I hear, the Irish got a hold of it."

I ran a hand through my hair. "Fuck."

Jacob nodded in agreement. "Ben sold the brothel to Raven, and he left a big debt behind and split town."

I scoffed. "Some friend. How much does she owe the Irish?"

"Hard to tell. I don't have many connections there."

It was all starting to make sense. The Irish were ruthless. The fact that they'd let her go this long without paying was a surprise in itself. They had no morals and no respect within the organization; it was all about money. Cosa Nostra was built on family while the Irish was built on greed.

"Anything else you need me to do?" Jacob asked.

"Track down the friend. I want to pay him a little visit."

I really wanted to punch his teeth in for putting Raven in this situation. Jacob wrote something down in the small notepad before we shook hands. I stayed seated in the booth as Jacob left. The staff would be here soon to open up the diner for business.

I ran a hand over my face. It was all starting to make sense, but why didn't she just tell me? She knew who I was. I could've taken care of this before it got out of hand. I wonder what the Irish thought of one of my enforcers standing guard outside of their business. Raven's been dealt a shitty hand of cards ever since she was born. She probably saw the brothel as her way out, her one chance at peace, and that man swiped the rug from under her before she could even get her footing. She's never had anyone to look after her. That's probably why she hadn't come to me. Everyone she put trust in screwed her over. Her foster parents kicked her out, her friend lied to her face.

I drummed my fingers against the table.

I had to do something. I wasn't going to kill her, but I couldn't exactly send her on her way back to the lion's den.

I'd have to buy the brothel from the Irish and pay off the debt Raven owns. Take ownership of the place, just like all my other businesses. Raven could still run the brothel how she wanted. I'd take a small cut of the profits and promise protection. It would be like any other business deal.

The bell to the door chimed, and I turned around to see Tommy walking into the diner. He wore a full suit with his hair gelled back.

"What are you doing here?" I asked.

Tommy sat down across from me at the table. "I heard what happened last night. Took a while for me to find you."

Out of all the capos, I was closest to Tommy, even though we couldn't be more different.

While I was always on the go, Tommy was very private and laid back. He flew under the radar as much as possible. He handled problems on his own and rarely asked for help.

"Didn't know anyone was looking for me."

"Bullshit. What's going on? Where's the girl?" Tommy asked, his eyes narrowed in concern.

If there's one thing Tommy didn't stand for, it's putting hands on a woman. Something about his dad beating his mom when he was younger.

"Calm down. She's at the apartment curled up with my dog."

He let out a sigh of relief and relaxed into the chair. "So what now?"

"I don't know. She's in some deep shit with the Irish. They own the brothel...I'm thinking about buying it."

He lifted an eyebrow. "Really? You just met this girl. Is she worth getting tied up with those goons?"

I'd asked myself the same thing, but I couldn't let her go knowing the damage the Irish would do to her when she didn't have their money.

"I don't know," I admitted.

Chapter Fifteen

<u>Raven</u>

After Enzo left, I went back to sleep for a couple hours and then decided it was time to pull myself together. I'm alive, he hadn't killed me, but I had to figure a way out of this mess. I took a shower and changed into a long sleeve dress. Not long after Enzo left, Cal came through the front door and dropped a bag of clothes and toiletries on the kitchen table without a word. I was grateful because the last thing I want to do was wear Enzo's clothes.

I felt better once my face wasn't caked in dried tears and makeup. Bello followed me around the house as I got ready like I was actually going somewhere, though I knew full well that I was trapped.

I didn't even have my phone to call Erica and let her know I was safe. What if the Irish come back while I was gone? No, Enzo said he still had his guard at the door. But would that really keep them out? Would Enzo really make an effort to protect my business? A week ago, I might had said yes, but with everything going on now, I didn't know anymore. I had no idea what he was thinking. He probably saw me as a thief and nothing more. I hated the way it made my heart ache.

I walked around the apartment, exploring the rooms I hadn't seen yet. The one next to the master bedroom was his office. There was a black desk in the center. It had that rustic look to it like the rest of the apartment. I should've closed the door, but something drew me inside. I took a step into the room, expecting Bello to follow behind me, but he laid down outside the door, like he knew we weren't supposed to be in there. I wondered how much time Enzo actually spent in the office. From the short amount of time I've been around him, it didn't seem like he was someone to sit at a desk for hours on end. The floor creaked as I crossed the room to the desk. I ran my hand over the smooth surface. The rest of the room was pretty empty. There wasn't any books or piles of paperwork, just one built in shelf behind the desk that held a wooden decorative toolbox, two fake plants, and a wire basket with nothing in it. He must've had an interior designer decorate the place because I couldn't imagine him picking out these items on his own.

"Stealing and snooping?"

I jumped at his deep voice, turning to see him leaning against the door frame. He wore the same clothes he left the house in hours earlier.

I shrugged, trying to appear casual. "You left me alone."

He scoffed. "You have an excuse for everything, don't you?"

I narrowed my eyes at him and crossed my arms over my chest. "If you aren't going to kill me, why are you keeping me here?"

He raised an eyebrow. "Why do you think I'm not going to kill you?"

"Because you would have done it already."

When he killed that man at the brothel, he hadn't thought twice. If he'd planned to kill me, it would already be done.

He pushed off the wall and walked out the door. "Don't flatter yourself."

I followed after him into his bedroom, where he sat on the edge of the bed. I opened my mouth, but he beat me to it.

"I know why you took the money," he said as he removed one shoe and let it drop on the floor with a thud.

"I told you I didn't have a choice."

"You could have told me," he said, looking up to see my reaction. I tried to keep my facial expression under control. I could've told him, but that would have been an even bigger risk. If he'd turned me away, I would have had no way to get the money.

He sighed, untied his other shoe, and let it drop before he walked into the en suite bathroom and closed the door. I stood there for a minute until I heard the sound of the water going. Without thinking too much about it, I barged into the bathroom. He stood under the water, letting it run over his hair. The muscles in his back looked even more ripped as the water ran down every crevice. He must have heard me come in, but he didn't react. I swallowed, trying not to get sidetracked by his hard ass. I could bounce a quarter off that ass.

"If you know I had to steal from you, that I didn't have another choice, why am I here? Thirty-thousand dollars is nothing to you." I waved my hand around, indicating the apartment. "Why don't you just let me go?"

He turned to face me, his dick at full attention. I quickly averted my attention back up to his face. At one point, I would have stripped down and got in the shower with him, but now, all I could see was red.

"If you aren't going to get in with me, you can get out," he said. His voice didn't come out harsh. It sounded more like he was stating a fact. Did he really want me to get in with him? Even after all that had happened last night? Not giving it too much thought, I walked away from him and slammed the bathroom door shut.

*****

I sat on the couch with Bello next to me as I flipped through the channels on the TV. It had been so long since I watched television, I don't even recognize any of the shows. I landed on a medical mystery show and tried to forget about the situation I was in. What I really needed was a drink. Maybe I could raid Enzo's cabinets later and come up with a concoction. It's nearly five o'clock, so it's not too early for a cocktail.

After the strange shower encounter last night, I slept on the couch with Bello. This was starting to become my favorite place in the apartment. I still didn't understand what Enzo's game was. He hasn't killed me so why keep me here? Bello's head popped up in curiosity, then a knock sounded at the front door. I jumped at the unexpected noise but didn't make a move to open it. It wasn't my house, anyways. Plus, I'm sure one of the many large men that take orders from Enzo was standing guard. A moment later, the doorknob turned, and a young girl poked her head inside. She couldn't be more than sixteen.

I sat up straight on the couch.

"Bello," the girl called, taking a step inside. Bello jumped off the couch and raced toward the door. Well, if Bello deemed the stranger safe, I guess I could too. I stood up and followed behind Bello.

"Oh hello. Sorry, I wasn't expecting anyone to be here," the girl said, her cheeks turned a bright red. She was dressed in a pair of purple yoga pants and a loose tank top.

"I'm Raven."

The girl gave me a tight-lipped smile. "Morgan...um, is Enzo here?"

"Unfortunately," I grumbled.

Morgan grabbed the leash off the hook. Bello was already sitting at her feet, wagging his tail. So this must be the dog walker. I was surprised Enzo trusted a teenager to come into his apartment. She twirled the leash between her fingers as if trying to think of something to say. Enzo choose that moment to walk out of his bedroom.

"Hi, Enzo," Morgan said, the redness in her cheeks deepened. I couldn't help but smirk as I realized the reason for the girl's nervousness. She had a crush on him. He stopped next to me and put an arm around my waist. His hand landed on a patch of open skin, and my body instantly reacted as if remembering how good his hands could feel.

"I didn't know you'd be home. I was just taking Bello out for his walk."

Enzo flashed her a smile, putting on the charm that I'd been stupid enough to fall for at one point.

"It's fine. Usually, I wouldn't be home, but I had something to attend to. Thanks for taking him."

The girl nodded, quickly fastened the leash to Bello, and walked out the door. Enzo immediately dropped his arm from around me, and it was like I could breathe again. He waltzed into the kitchen.

"You know, I could have told her that you were holding me hostage," I said.

He opened the fridge and leaned down to see what was inside.

"That would have put her in a really awkward situation," he replied, not even sparing me a glance.

"You make her nervous."

He straightened and leaned against the counter. "No, I don't."

"Yes, you do. That girl has a little crush on you."

Enzo frowned. "Oh." He seemed surprised by the statement. How did he not realize it?

"There's nothing to eat in this house," he said after a moment.

"Yeah, that's what happens when you only use your apartment to sleep."

I started walking back to the living room area to return to watching TV.

"I'm ordering Chinese food."

"Don't care," I responded.

Chapter Sixteen

<u>Enzo</u>

As I grabbed the bag of Chinese food from the delivery man, my phone started to ring. Work never fucking stops. I tip the guy what I think is a generous amount, but it's been so long since I've ordered take-out, I wasn't sure what was expected. Fifteen percent? Twenty percent? After closing the door, I set the bags down on the island and pulled out my phone.

"Enzo," I answered.

"I'll have a clear shot in about twenty minutes as long as I have your go-ahead," Cole said.

With all the bullshit that's been going on, I'd completely forgot that Cole was on a mission to take out a gang leader.

"Take the shot. Text me when you're done."

I hung up and placed the phone down on the island. Just as I was about to unpack the food, it rang again.

"What the fuck," I mumbled to myself. Business never stopped. Most of the time, I didn't mind. It kept me going. But now with Raven here, I just wanted a second of quiet. I have to figure out what the fuck to do about this whole brothel situation, and I can't do that if my phone keeps blowing up every two minutes.

"Hello."

"We got a problem over here, Boss," Cal said.

That doesn't sound good. Cal would only call if it was important. "Fuck, I'll be right there."

Raven walked into the kitchen dressed in a tight tank top and a pair of skimpy pajama shorts. Her long legs are on display, and the tank top barely contains her tits. Is she doing this on purpose?

"What's going on?" she asked as I set the phone down before pulling my shoes on.

"I gotta go." I gave her a stern look. "Don't try to leave."

I'm out the door and in my car in a matter of minutes. I waste no time speeding down the New York streets to the brothel. Before I'd even parked the car, I knew why Cal called me. Three men dressed in suits stand on the stoop, looking just as pissed off as Cal. I threw the car in park and jogged up to the stoop.

"Do we have a problem here, boys?" I asked to add in extra insult.

I'm relieved that I don't recognize them. They didn't rank high enough for me to be familiar. Maybe this wasn't a high priority to the Irish.

One of the men smiled and took a step closer to me. My hand twitched for the gun that was tucked into my waistband.

"No problem at all. How about you just have your man move away from the door of *our* building and we won't have any problems." He opened his vest, flashing me the metal strapped to the side of his body.

"That's not going to happen."

Another one of the men stepped forward, but the main guy put a hand on his chest.

"There are a lot of witnesses around for you to be throwing threats like that," I said.

He looked around as if just now noticing all the people on the street. A woman and her young child crossed the road. The mailman dropped a package on the stoop two houses down. I could really give a fuck about the witnesses. Cosa Nostra had enough cops on our payroll to cover up nearly everything, but the Irish didn't. They're goldfish, and I'm a goddamn shark.

"What's your name?" he asked.

"Enzo."

He nodded. "We'll be in touch, Enzo."

They walked down the stairs to a black car parked out front.

Now I had a target on my back and I'm not too fond of that feeling. My mind wanders back to Raven. I'm risking a lot for her and I still don't know why. Yes, she's beautiful and her bad attitude turned me on. Was that reason enough to risk my life?

I walked up the steps and into the brothel. Erica sat at the front desk. She must be taking Raven's place. She stands to her feet as I close the door.

"Where's Raven?" she snapped, her hands going to her hips. I'm amused by her confidence, especially since she has seen me kill a man in this very building.

I smirked at her. "Alive."

Her shoulders visibly relax. Erica must have known what Raven set out to do when she left the brothel the other night.

"She won't be back for a while," I added.

Erica's eyes narrowed. "What do you mean? What the fuck have you done to her?"

I furrowed my eyebrows at the suggestion that I hurt her, but I shouldn't be surprised. That's the reputation I needed to uphold anyways. It's better if people believe I'm a monster. Fewer people try to cross me that way...the exception being Raven.

"I swear to god if you hurt her—"

"Then what?" I challenged.

"I'll kill you my damn self. You might think she just runs this place, but she's family. She has helped all of us in ways that we could never repay her for, so if that means going against you, I wouldn't hesitate."

I'm speechless. Erica's a prostitute at Raven's brothel, but she thinks of Raven as family. I don't know a lot about the business, but I doubt many prostitutes would refer to their madam or pimp as family. From what I knew about Raven, though, she had a bigger heart than most people probably realized. She isn't greedy or money hungry like other people in the business. The front door opened, and a man dressed in a tight suit walks in.

"I'll have Raven call you," I tell her before walking past the man and back out to the sidewalk.

"Everything good?" Cal asked. He stood next to the building like a bouncer at a nightclub. I shook my head. Nothing was good. Everything was going to shit. There's only one way I saw to get out of this situation.

I'd have to buy the brothel from the Irish. I could add it to my lineup of other businesses. Raven could continue running the place how she wanted. With my protection and the Irish off her back, she'd have nothing to worry about, but I'd have to fix the money issue. The prostitutes were probably getting paid more than Raven was, and that wasn't going to fly.

"I'm adding another man to the watch. Let me know if anything else happens," I said to Cal.

"Yes, Boss."

*****

When I got back to the apartment, I found Raven in the guest bedroom. She sat up against the headboard. Her long red hair fell over her shoulders, covering her exposed skin. Her skin was perfect. Her nipples poked through the tight tank top, and my dick twitched at the sight. Fuck, I wanted to bury myself inside her again.

"Can I help you?" she snapped. I directed my eyes away from her breast and back to her face.

"You're eating with me. Come on."

She raised an eyebrow. "And why would I do that?"

"Maybe because I'm the only thing standing between your girls and the Irish taking them and selling them on the black market."

Her features softened as the truth hit her. If it wasn't for me, the girls would probably already be sex slaves to some sick bastard that got off on that kind of thing. Reluctantly, she climbed off the bed and followed behind me to the kitchen. She sat at the island as I warmed up the Chinese food for both of us. I grabbed two forks from the drawer and handed her the box of rice before sitting across from her with my food.

"Thanks," she mumbled.

I nodded, and we ate our food in awkward silence.

"So what's your plan?" she asked me.

"For what?"

"For everything. When can I go back to the house?"

I shrugged. "I'll let you know when you can go back. My plan right now is to buy the business from the Irish."

Her eyes widened in shock like a deer in the headlights. "Why would you do that?"

I tilted my head, trying to figure out what she meant.

"So I'm going from one mafia to another?" she asked.

"You've been lucky so far. You can't run a business like that in the Bronx by yourself. You need protection."

I was surprised this was the first time she has had any major issues. Raven was tough, but she wasn't shit compared to the bad men out there in the underground world. The Irish were only the tip of the iceberg. If other people found out that a woman was running the brothel with no other outside protection, they wouldn't hesitate to take it over.

"So, I'd have to give you a cut of my profits? Just like the Irish?"

"We'll talk about it once I buy it."

She pushed her food away from her. "You realize you're putting me in the same situation I've been trying to get out of, right? I don't want someone else to own *my* business."

"It would still be your business. You can still run it, but the house will belong to me...to Cosa Nostra. We'll control the money and the security."

"Are you fucking kidding me? So I'm just supposed to be like an employee?"

I shrugged again. "If that's how you want to think about it."

She glared at me from across the island. Her eyes flashed with hatred, but it didn't bother me in the least. I'm doing what's right for her even if she doesn't want to see it. The brothel could make way more money, and I could stabilize the business if I owned it.

"I didn't get involved in this business so that I could collect a paycheck. Why do you need me if that's your plan?"

"Would you want me to put someone else in your position?" I challenged. That isn't what she wants. Raven had a soft spot for the women, and she wouldn't turn her back and let someone else run the place. I walked around the island to stand next to her. The scent of vanilla filled my nose. She looked up at me from the stool. Her eyes held a mixture of confusion and stress. I realized it's the lack of control that bothers her. The idea of me owning the business terrified her. She didn't trust me, and she had no reason to yet. I'd have to prove to her that she can trust me. There's something about this woman that made me want to earn her trust. We could run this business together like a king and queen. She could still do what she's been doing, but no one would dare cross her unless they had a death wish. She would have all the respect in the world with me on her side.

"We can make this work if you would stop resisting," I said.

"Resisting? You're talking about taking my business." Her hand twitched like she wanted to slap me.

"No, I'm talking about buying a business from the Irish. You never owned it."

Her eyes flickered away from me back down to the table. Her shoulders slumped down as she accepted that she didn't have any other option.

"I want to be able to make decisions. My girls should be able to keep most of their money."

"We'll talk about it." There's no way in hell the girls would keep the same percentage they're currently keeping, but I didn't feel like arguing about it right now.

"I should go to bed," she said.

I looked at the clock on the wall. It's three a.m., which is probably early for her. Still, it's just an excuse to get away from me. My eyes flicker to her breasts again, and I imagine her in my bed with her tits pressed against me. My dick hardens at the thought.

"You can always sleep in my bed," I offer. As if on cue, she looks down at my crouch. The outline of my dick is obvious. She pulls her bottom lip into her mouth as if thinking about it. She has a war going on inside her. She hates me but wants me at the same time. Instead of hearing her rejection, I turn and walk to my bedroom.

*****

"I heard you have a bit of a situation," Giovanni said, sitting across from me at his dining room table.

"I need to buy the brothel from the Irish," I blurted out. I had to get the go-ahead from Giovanni before making a move. If this was a regular business, it would be no problem, but since another organization had been thrown into the mix, I had to cover all my bases.

Giovanni was already shaking his head. "No way in hell. We just squashed a lot of shit with the Irish. I'm not going to start anything with them. I want some distance between the two of us for a while."

Damn, I should have saw that coming. Tommy did warn me about Cosa Nostra's recent issues with the Irish.

"I need to buy it. Raven—"

"Raven?" he asked, narrowing his dark eyes on me. "This is because of a girl? I thought you just wanted to expand some of your business. I'm not poking at the Irish because of a girlfriend." He let out a grunt as if annoyed that I'd even asked him in the first place. He leaned back in the chair and lit a blunt. I clenched my fists under the table, trying not to show my irritation. I had to buy this brothel from the Irish or else Raven would be shit out of luck. There was no other options. Then, an idea popped in my head.

"What about a wife?" I asked.

Giovanni froze. "Excuse me?"

"What if my wife was in danger?"

Giovanni stared me down and a shiver ran down my spine. I had to tread very carefully. Wives of made men were held with the utmost respect. Even after a made man died, we continued to take care of widows. After my father died, my mother needed the help that Cosa Nostra gave. She never had to worry a day in her life. Was I really willing to give that sort of opportunity to Raven? Right now, she hated my guts. Our relationship was far from what most people would consider romantic.

"Wives have a different status, you know that. If you had a wife that was in danger, it would be considered a personal issue for us."

I stood up from the table and started to walk away.

"Don't do anything stupid," Giovanni called after me, but it was too late.

Chapter Seventeen

I stood by the fridge and unloaded bags of groceries. One of Enzo's men had taken my grocery list and picked up what I needed. I'd just set the bottle of ketchup down when the door slammed. I jumped, almost hitting my head on the top of the fridge. Turning around, I saw Enzo standing in the doorway.

"What the hell?!" I snapped.

"We're getting married."

I opened my mouth and closed it again. Open. Close. Like a fish trying to get water. What the fuck did he just say to me?

"Excuse me?" I must have misheard him. That's what it is. I've been cooped up in this apartment so long, I'm hearing things.

"Pack a bag. We're leaving tomorrow morning," he said. He crossed his arms over his chest, and if I wasn't so shocked by his words, I might be able to admire how damn good the veins in his forearms looked right now.

I blinked a few times to clear my head. *Focus, Raven, this man just said we're getting married.* "I'm not getting married to you. Are you out of your mind?!" I said, finally finding my voice. I never wanted to get married, much less to someone I barely knew.

"It wasn't a question, and if you want this little situation to get handled, then you will need a ring on your finger."

How the hell would getting married right now help my situation? The Irish could be storming into the brothel any day now to try to take my girls and he wanted to throw a wedding?

"I never asked for your help," I reminded him.

"You didn't have to. Pack a bag."

He turned to walk away and I followed after him. "How is getting married supposed to help my situation?" I followed him into his office where he sat down at the desk.

"If we're married, you have a level of protection with Cosa Nostra. You're considered one of our own, and we take care of our own. Which means they'll back me up when it comes to making sure the Irish keep their greedy hands off of your brothel."

I crossed my arms over my chest as I allowed everything to sink in. I didn't want to get married, but that was a small price to pay to make sure my girls were taken care of. I couldn't imagine them getting taken just because I refused to put a ring on my finger.

"So what happens after the Irish are taken care of? We get divorced?"

Enzo shook his head. "Catholics don't get divorced."

Anger took over my body. "Are you fucking kidding me? I'm going to be married to you forever? You think I'm going to live here like some housewife?"

He didn't respond, just stared at me with an expression I was unable to read. I turned and started to walk out of the office. I was barely holding on to my temper.

"Pack a bag," he repeated. I flipped him the bird before slamming the door to his office. I felt like an angry child, but I didn't care. This was the rest of my life he was talking about. I sat at the kitchen island with my hands on my head. Was I really going to do this? Get married to a stranger so that I could save the brothel? I didn't really have a choice at this point. Enzo would marry me anyways, even if it meant paying someone to file the paperwork and forging my signature. I had never before imagined a wedding day because I never imagined getting married. Women like me didn't get married. That was for women who grew up with two parents and a white picket fence, not me, who bounced from foster home to foster home.

If I really had to imagine myself at a wedding ceremony, I'd imagine that Erica and the other girls from the house and Toby would be there. Those were the only people I cared about, but it didn't matter. It wasn't a real wedding anyways. I took a deep breath and squared my shoulders. If I could risk my life counting cards, then I could suck it up and marry Enzo.

*****

"Where are we going?" I asked as we waited in line at the airport.

"To get married," he said as if it was the most obvious thing in the world.

"Wow, thanks."

His lips lifted into the hint of a smile. "We're going somewhere you've never been."

"Well, considering I've barely left New York besides to smuggle drugs, that leaves a lot of options."

The older woman in front us turned around to stare at me.

"Can I help you?" I barked. She quickly turned back around.

Enzo looked at me out the corner of his eye but didn't say anything. We moved through security. Enzo was somehow able to get me a passport overnight. He'd dressed in a pair of dark jeans and a button-down shirt. He looked good in anything he wore, but I liked it best when he was in a pair of sweatpants with no shirt on. I followed him through the airport before taking a seat at our gate.

"Are you inviting anyone?" I asked him. He mentioned his mom once, and I wonder if he'd invite her.

"My mom and sister are meeting us down there." He handed over my plane ticket. When I looked down, I had to double check to make sure I read it right.

"Italy?"

"My mom said she's always imagined me getting married there."

I guess Italy is as good a place as any to get married. "I've never been."

"It's beautiful. I think you'll like it." Butterflies started to form in my stomach. Even though this was under very strange circumstances, I couldn't hide that I was filled with both excitement and nerves. What would his mom think of me? Why did I care? His mom couldn't be happy that he was marrying a woman she hadn't even gotten the chance to meet yet.

"Is your mom going to hate me?"

"No, she'll love you. She will just be happy I'm getting married."

"Does she know—"

"No. And you're not going to tell her." He leveled me with a glare.

I looked away from him, out the window, and watched the planes land. I couldn't believe I was on my way to Italy to get married to Enzo. Even though I hated him right now for taking me prisoner and, now, forcing me to be his wife, there were worse men I could spend the rest of my life with. Working at the brothel, I've been surrounded by men who didn't have respect for anything or anyone. Enzo was far from the worst. He was getting married in Italy to please his mom—that must count for something.

"Come on," he said, bringing me out of my thoughts. The plane had started to board. He carried my small carry-on bag to our seat and placed it in the overhang. We were seated in first class. At least that's what I assumed since the seats looked more spread out than I imagined and the people already seated had glasses of champagne in their hands.

"Can I sit by the window?" I asked him. He nodded and I slid into the seat. My stomach clenched a moment when I realized how far away from the ground the plane was, and we weren't even in the sky yet.

"Nervous?" he whispered into my ear. Goosebumps rose over my body as I nodded my head.

"Have you ever been on a plane?" he asked.

"No, plane tickets are expensive." I looked around at the area we were seated in. I had a ton of room to stretch out, and there was a TV to one side of me. There was also a short plastic wall that gave us some privacy from the rest of the passengers. Enzo got into the seat next to me and pulled out his phone. The flight attendant stood at the front of the aircraft and started to go over the safety features as I felt the plane move. I looked out the window and saw we were slowly rolling toward the runway. The flight attendant finished her speech, and we started to gain speed. My stomach twisted, and I gripped the side of the seat.

Enzo reached over and, to my surprise, grabbed one of my hands and squeezed.

"Taking off is the worst part. Once we're in the sky, it levels out."

I squeezed my eyes shut as I felt the plane lift off the ground.

"Can we get a couple glasses of champagne?" Enzo said to someone. A moment later, a glass was placed in my hand. I opened my eyes to look down at the champagne.

"It will help you to relax."

I nodded and drank it all down in one go. He handed me another one, and I managed to smile at him.

Once we were in the sky, I started to relax a little bit. I was able to look out the window and see all the clouds and houses below them.

"You will love Italy. It's beautiful," Enzo said.

"You've been before?" I asked.

He nodded. "A few times."

I imagined Enzo would blend in perfectly in a place like Italy.

"Sleep. We have a long time before we land."

I snuggled down in the seat and let my eyes close.

*****

Light coming through the small window woke me up. I squinted out the window and turned in the seat to see Enzo typing away on his phone.

"Did you sleep at all?" I said as I sat up.

"You slept long enough for both of us. We'll be landing soon."

The seatbelt light came on, and the pilot came over the speaker, letting us know we were descending.

"Is your mom there already?" I asked Enzo.

"No, she'll be here tonight."

The time zone change was already throwing me off. It was still bright and sunny in Italy. The landing wasn't as bad as take-off, but Enzo still interlocked his fingers with mine when I'd gripped the chair. It was a small gesture, but it was the most affection I'd seen out of him in a while. If I was honest, the feeling of his hand against mine made me want to run my hand over his chest. I missed the feeling of his body against me, but I reminded myself that I was being taken prisoner right now. He was forcing me to marry him and fly to another country when I should be finding a way to protect my girls. The scent of his cologne filled my nose as he got up and grabbed my bag from the overhang.

"You didn't pack anything?" I asked, realizing for the first time that he hadn't brought a bag.

"No, everything I need is at the house."

"House?" I asked.

He winked at me. "You'll see."

We got off the plane and walked through the airport. When we got outside, it was like the air felt lighter. I noticed everyone moved slower too. There weren't many people rushing around to catch their plane. I could tell already that I was going to like Italy. A cab was already waiting for us at the curb. Once inside, I looked out the window as the beautiful city passed us by. The architecture was amazing. Great detail and work were put into every single building. The churches were gigantic and took up the entire block. People walked and biked along the cobblestone streets. We drove through the city until we were far away from the beautiful buildings and people. My view from the window changed to miles of flowers and grass, the greenest grass I'd ever seen. Living in New York, the closer thing to grass I saw was in Central Park, and it was dying by this time of year.

"Beautiful, isn't it?" Enzo whispered in my ear. His deep voice was a straight shot to my core. Just looking at the scenery and feeling his breath on my neck instantly calmed me. I was safe here...with him.

"Gorgeous."

After a long drive, we pulled up to a stunning house. It looked to be at least two stories with a red roof and stucco siding. It definitely matched the rest of the landscape. Enzo got out first and paid the cab driver before opening my door. I followed after him into the home. The tall double wooden doors opened into a grand foyer. The inside of the house was luxurious, completely opposite of his apartment in the city. The walls were painted a dark beige and exposed wood beams complimented the high ceilings. There was also a feeling of warmness to the home despite its size.

"I'll show you to your room."

Lost for words, I simply followed behind him up a staircase. The room he showed me was decorated very feminine with a light pink comforter and sheer white curtains that allowed the sunlight to come through. I loved the brightness that the sun brought in. I walked toward the arched window and opened it to let the fresh air in. The breeze blew through my hair, and I took a long, deep breath. It was like after living so many years in the dark streets of New York, I was finally at peace here.

Enzo stood in the middle of the room with his hands in his pockets. "My room is next door. You're welcome anywhere in the house or on the property, but don't go too far—"

"There's a pool?" I asked, catching the sigh of water from the corner of my eye.

He smiled.

"I didn't bring a bathing suit." I don't even remember the last time I swam. I think it might have been when I lived with Toby's family as a kid. They had a lake house that we went to once.

"I'll get one for you." He turned to walk out of the room.

"Thank you," I said, stopping him in his tracks. I shouldn't be thanking him. I should be mad at him, but I couldn't help but feel grateful to be able to see the beauty of Italy. I never would have been outside the country if it weren't for him.

He nodded and walked out of the room. Once he left, I took a shower in my en suite bathroom. There were a couple big windows in there that faced the vast land that the house sat on. I opened those windows too. My body craved fresh air that wasn't filled with the stench of trash or the sound of homeless people arguing on the sidewalk. After my shower, I changed into some comfortable clothes. I walked out of the room to explore the house and ran into Cal in the hallway. He held a shopping bag out.

"Thank you."

He grunted in response.

"Do you ever talk?" I ask. Cal was the only one of Enzo's men that I knew by name. He guarded the apartment door sometimes when Enzo was gone, and he usually brought me the shit I needed.

Cal shrugged. "If needed."

I looked inside to find a bathing suit and a couple outfits. A genuine smile tugged at my lips, and I turned away from Cal to head back to my room. I put the bathing suit on under my clothes before emerging again. The door to Enzo's room was shut, and I wondered if he was finally sleeping. It seemed like he was always on the go. I rarely saw him relax. Walking past his door, I came across another room. The door was ajar, so I pushed it so it creaked open. It was an office, similar to the one Enzo had in his apartment. I walked back out, went down the staircase, and took a left. I found a huge kitchen with top-of-the-line appliances, as well as a dining room that could fit at least thirty people. I felt like a princess living in a castle, but Enzo was no Prince Charming, and I had to remind myself that I was being forced to marry him.

Chapter Eighteen

Looking out the window of my room, I watched as Raven peeled off her clothes to reveal the black bikini underneath. My dick hardened as I ran my eyes from her long legs up to her chest. I was going to have to thank Cal later for picking out the swimsuit. It left little to the imagination. I imagined wrapping my arms around her perfectly curved waist. This woman was going to be my wife, so I had the rest of my life to admire her body. Even though I was marrying her so she'd have Cosa Nostra's protection, I couldn't deny that I liked the idea of being fused to her for the rest of our lives. I wanted a claim on the woman who so desperately didn't want to be claimed. She sat at the edge of the pool, letting her legs dangle in the water. Fuck, I wanted to join her, but she probably needed some space. I had just flown her across the country to marry me. I let out a sigh and walked away from the window, my dick fully at attention. I was going to have to jack off in the shower later.

I never imagined getting married, but to my mom's delight, that's exactly what I was doing. After I took care of her brothel, I wondered if she would go back to running it, and if she would want to live with me or if it would be like this little thing between us never happened. Even if that's how we ended up, living two separate lives, I'll be happy that she at least enjoyed Italy as much as she already has. She wasn't the easiest person to read, but I'd picked up on that. A knock sounded on my door. I answered it to see Cal standing on the other side.

"Your mom's plane should be landing in four hours."

"Thanks."

"You need anything else, Boss?" Cal asked.

"I'm good. Just keep an eye on Raven, will ya?"

"Absolutely."

I closed the door. Four hours was just enough time to get some sleep. My body was begging me to rest, and I usually ignored it, but today, I decided to give in. I stripped off my clothes and got into the soft bed.

*****

I woke in a panic, searching for something…I'm not sure what, but my eyes scanned the blankets. That's when I realized the room was pitch black. I rubbed a hand over my face. Shit.

I grabbed my phone off the bedside table to check the time. It was nine o'clock. I'd slept the entire day. I quickly got into the shower and changed into a pair of sweatpants and a T-shirt before leaving the room. The sound of laughter echoed off the walls and floated to my floor. What the hell? I followed the sound to the dining room table where my mom and Raven were seated at the table. Raven's hair was piled on top of her head like she'd thrown it up after her swim. She was dressed in one of my T-shirts and pajama pants. Had she packed one of my shirts in her carry-on bag?

"Oh, look who's up," my mom teased. She was also dressed for bed, with a cup of steaming tea warming her hands. I bent down and kissed her cheek.

"How was your flight?" I asked.

She waved me off. "It was fine. I was just catching your fiancée up on all your embarrassing stories."

I rolled my eyes. "Great."

My mom has probably been waiting for this opportunity my whole life. She stood up from the table and placed her cup in the sink.

"I'm heading off to bed." She wrapped me in a tight hug, then squeezed Raven's shoulder. "You are going to make a beautiful bride." She said before leaving us in the kitchen.

I sat down in the chair my mom had vacated. Raven and I were close enough to touch, and I wanted to run my hand over her soft skin to feel the goosebumps that would rise with my touch, but she had to be the one to reach out, to beg for me to touch her.

"Your mom is nice."

I shrugged. "She's been wanting me to get married for a long time. I think she'd almost given up hope."

"Doesn't she find this a little odd? That I just came out of nowhere?"

"My mom was married to a made man for many years. She has learned not to ask questions."

Raven raised her eyebrow at me. "Is that what you think I'm going to do once we're married? Not ask questions?"

I smiled. Raven could never be the typical mob wife. "No. You are already a part of this world. I can't stop you from asking about my businesses."

She looked down at the table. "Why are we getting married?"

"For your protection."

"I know, but why do you care so much? You could have just killed me. Or let me figure out everything on my own. Why are you helping me?" She lifted her eyes up to stare into mine.

"I don't know." I tried to think of an explanation. I wouldn't do this for anyone else, but I felt something for Raven that I've never felt for anyone else. I wanted to be her savior for some reason. That first night I saw her at the underground, I just wanted to get her on her back, but as time went on, it grew into something stronger. Any other woman in her situation would jump at the opportunity for me to help her, but Raven was fighting me every step of the way. Maybe it was because I wanted to show her that she could trust me. "I can't walk away knowing that no one has ever taken care of you."

Her lip twitched like she wanted to smile. I didn't feel good about forcing her into a marriage, but I needed to protect her. No one had ever fought for her or even helped her. I wanted to be that person for her. The person she could lean on when life got too heavy.

"I should probably get some sleep," she said.

"I'll see you in the morning."

She got up from the chair, but before walking away, she bent down and pressed her plump lips to mine. The kiss was soft but heated. Too soon, she pulled away and I heard the sound of footsteps climbing the stairs.

I sat at the table for a minute in the silence. It was evening in New York, and I didn't have anything urgent to get to. The quiet and stillness was uncomfortable. I was never still. I always had something to do, someone to talk to, business to handle. I paced the kitchen for a while before opening the fridge and pulling out leftover pasta that my mom and Raven must've made for dinner. After eating, my body started to feel tired again despite all the hours I'd slept, but I didn't want to go back to my room alone. I climbed the stairs and slowly opened Raven's bedroom door. The creaking sound it made must have woken her up, but she didn't stir. The only light in the room came through the window from the moon. I walked across the floor and got under the covers. The bed dipped with my weight, but she still didn't move. She might turn around and tell me to get out, but I was hoping she wouldn't. After a minute of no movement from her, I wrapped my arms around her and pulled her soft body to my hard chest. I waited until her breathing evened out before allowing myself to close my eyes and fall asleep too.

Chapter Nineteen

<u>Raven</u>

His arms wrapped tightly around me. I vaguely remembered him coming into the bedroom last night. I couldn't help relaxing into his embrace. It felt so right, but everything surrounding us was so wrong. In a matter of hours, Enzo would be my husband. This all felt like a dream...or a nightmare. I wasn't sure which one yet. I'm unsure about everything, except the man lying next to me. There was one consistency in all of this, and that was him. He didn't have an ulterior motive other than to help me for reasons I still didn't understand. I'd pushed him away time and time again, but he never wavered. Maybe it was time to start trusting him. It was easier said than done, but he'd done nothing to earn my distrust. He didn't have to put his neck on the line to save my girls, but he did it anyways. It would have been easy for him to walk away as if he'd never met me, but he didn't. A pressure against my back brought me back to the present.

Is that...? Oh yeah, it's definitely his hard dick digging into my ass cheek. He didn't move, but he had to be awake. I had two options: get out of bed like nothing had happened or provoke the beast. His arms tightened around me, and my decision was made. I ground my ass against his hard cock. It had been too long since I'd been underneath him and every inch of my body craved his touch. The slight roughness of his five-o'clock shadow tickled my neck as he moved his mouth to my ear and nibbled on it. No words needed to be spoken between us. He moved his hand between my legs and rubbed circles over the pajama bottoms. I couldn't help moving my hips to get more contact. Wetness gathered between my thighs, and as if reading my mind, he slipped his hand underneath the pants and into my panties.

"Fuck, you're so wet," he groaned. His voice was deep and husky, like he was struggling to keep himself contained. He grabbed on to my hips and flipped me over so I lay on my back with my legs spread open enough so he could settle in-between them. He hovered over me, his elbows on the bed for balance. I reached under his shirt, feeling the outline of every single one of his abs. His body was perfectly molded, as if he's been training for battle. His green eyes stared into mine, searching for something. Maybe he was looking for my hesitation. He wouldn't find any. I wanted him. I've always wanted him, no matter how much I tried to hate him. Just to show him how much I wanted him, I grabbed the waistband of his pants and pushed them down so that his beautiful dick was on full display, big, veiny, and with a shiny spot of pre-cum at the tip. I craved the feeling of him stretching me wide.

"In a few hours, you're going to be my wife," he said.

"Then fuck me like a husband," I challenged.

The corner of his mouth twitched before he leaned down to touch his lips against mine. The kiss was so gentle, it caught me by surprise. I fisted his cock and slowly stroked him.

"Fuck," he moaned against my mouth. He broke the kiss and pulled my pants and panties off as if he couldn't get to me fast enough. In a matter of seconds, he was buried inside me, stretching me to the point where it was almost painful. His arms hooked underneath my legs, keeping me wide open for him. I felt so full, and my body was hot against his skin.

"Damn, baby, you feel so good."

He started to move, slowly at first, but I wanted more. Needed more. I grabbed onto his ass, pulling him into me as deep as he would go. He reached between us and rubbed my clit. As if he'd hit the launch button, my body started to tingle, and waves of pleasure overtook me. It was like my ears were stuffed with cotton as I came down from the high. My walls clenched around him, and he picked up his pace. The headboard slammed against the wall each time he thrusted into me until his muscles tightened and he found his own release.

*****

A man stood in the middle of the room, unzipping dresses and laying them out on the bed. They were all gorgeous, but one in particular caught my eye. It was a mermaid-style dress. The top was sleeveless and covered with lace that was intertwined to create beautiful designs.

"I want to try that one," I told the stylist. Enzo hired him to get me ready for the big day. I was only a couple hours away from meeting Enzo down in the garden. There weren't any big decorations down there, just an alter and one lone chair for Elizabeth, his mom, to sit. The stylist helped me get into the dress. It fit like a glove, sticking to every curve, and the neckline exhibited my breasts nicely. A knock sounded at the door before it opened a crack.

"Are you decent?" Elizabeth asked.

"Yes."

She walked the rest of the way into the room and her eyes widened as she saw the dress. "You look gorgeous."

I could't help but smile. "Thank you." I'd gotten to know Elizabeth well last night. I almost had a panic attack when she showed up at the house and Enzo was nowhere to be found, but she had immediately embraced me and told me how excited she was about the marriage. She'd showed me how to make one of her pasta dishes last night, and it turned out delicious. She was quiet and sweet but had a sarcastic sense of humor that made me laugh.

"Can we have a minute?" Elizabeth asked the stylist.

Once he was out of the room, she grabbed my hand and led me to a part of the bed that was not completely covered with the other wedding dress options.

"I know this isn't a traditional wedding," she said, catching me off guard. "I don't need to or want to know the details, but I want you to know that you are family now. His sister couldn't be here, but I'm sure Enzo will introduce you soon. We don't believe in divorce, so you're always family."

It was such a foreign concept to me. For someone who jumped from foster home to foster home, the closest thing I had to family was Toby, and even then, we weren't actually related or bound by a marriage. Elizabeth wiped away a single tear that escaped her eye.

"Thank you," I said.

Elizabeth nodded. "My son is a proud man...too proud. I only ask one thing of you."

I tensed up, preparing for what she was going to ask.

"Please make that man slow down."

We both laughed so loud, we didn't hear Enzo walk in the room. His eyes were glued to me.

"Get out! You aren't supposed to see the bride before the wedding!" His mom swatted at him.

"Okay, okay, I just needed to drop this off."

He pulled a small velvet box from his pocket and handed to me. I took it in my hands, feeling the smoothness of the velvet. I looked at both Elizabeth and Enzo before opening up the box. The ring inside was gorgeous. Small gemstones covered the platinum band, leading up to the prong setting that held the gigantic diamond. It was huge and would probably weigh down my finger. It was a statement. He wanted everyone to know that I belonged to him.

He cleared his throat. "I just wanted you to see it before the ceremony. I'll see you down there. Mother, will you bring it down to the alter when she's done?"

"Of course."

Once he left, I picked up the halo-shaped diamond and slid it on my finger. It was heavier than it looked. It would be a constant reminder of the vows we were about to share.

"It's gorgeous," Elizabeth said.

"It is," I agreed. I took the ring back off and placed it back in the box. Elizabeth bent down to kiss my forehead before leaving the room with my ring.

The stylist finished getting me ready. When he finished, I felt like a princess. My makeup was done perfectly, and my hair was twisted up in a curly updo. I barely recognized the woman staring back at me in the window. A knock sounded at the door before Cal peaked his head in.

"They're ready for you."

It was kind of silly to think about, how we got dressed up for only three people. Grabbing the skirt of my dress so it didn't drag on the floor, I followed Cal downstairs to the living room. The entire wall was actually a door that opened up to the backyard. Enzo stood next to a big maple tree, underneath an altar. His suit fit perfectly across his broad shoulders. His hair was combed back, and it looked soft, like I could easily run my hands through it. An older man stood next to Enzo with the Bible in his hand. Elizabeth turned around in her seat and gave me a big smile.

Cal cleared his throat and handed me a bouquet of red and white flowers.

"Thank you."

Music started to play—that was my cue. I dropped the skirt of my dress, gripped the bouquet in my hands, and started the walk to my husband. I walked alone, but I wasn't sad about it. If anything, it was a statement. No one was giving me away. All of this was my choice, even though it didn't feel like it. I didn't need someone else walking me down the aisle to give me away to the man that stood at the end. As I got closer to Enzo, there was a softness to his expression that I'd never seen before. He wasn't on guard like he usually was. For the first time, he actually looked relaxed. He took my hand as I stepped up to the altar and stood across from him. His eyes roamed over my body, taking in the dress that hugged my curves and the makeup that had been perfectly applied.

"You're so beautiful, baby," he whispered.

I smiled at him and the priest cleared his throat. "Ready?"

Enzo nodded. "We're ready."

The ceremony was quick. We repeated the vows that the priest told us to. Then, we went back into the house. It all felt kind of anti-climactic, almost like it wasn't real. I didn't feel any different as Enzo poured me and his mother a glass of wine and set it in front of us at the small table in the kitchen.

"Thank you, but I think I'll take this outside. I'm leaving in the morning and I want to enjoy Italy for a bit longer." Elizabeth excused herself and Enzo took her spot.

I lifted the glass up to my lips and took a sip. All of this was so out of character for me. If someone had told me a couple months ago that I'd be sitting in a mansion in Italy drinking wine across from my husband, I would have laughed in their face.

"What are you thinking about?" Enzo asked, taking a sip of what looked like cognac.

"This all feels...unreal. I never really imagined getting married."

"Me neither."

"Yeah?"

He took another sip before placing the glass down on the table. "My mom has been pestering for years to find someone. I never thought I would."

"But this isn't really a conventional marriage. I mean, this wouldn't have happened if it weren't for the trouble I'm in."

He shrugged. "Maybe not, but we're still married, and I expect this to be treated like any other marriage."

"What are you trying to say?" I ask.

His eyes narrowed on me. "I'm not sharing you with anybody."

I hadn't even thought about that. It's not like I was getting sex regularly before I hooked up with Enzo. Lots of men had mistresses, and Enzo probably had his fair share of women in the past.

"I want the same from you—"

"You don't even have to ask that."

I took a sip of my wine. "What about after you buy the brothel?"

If he was going to buy the brothel like he planned, then what would that mean for us? Would we just keep playing house or would I go back to my old life?

His jaw twitched like he was annoyed by the question. "You'll still be my wife."

"But—"

"But nothing. When you said those vows, you agreed to spend your life with me. You can do what you want with the brothel, but we're partners now, and we have a lot more businesses than yours to consider. We will run our businesses like king and queen, and you will come home to me every night."

We sat in silence as I allowed his words to sink in. Our marriage was necessary for him to buy the brothel, but I realized it wasn't just a step in the process. I made a commitment to him, to love him in sickness and in health, rich and poor. We were partners now in business but also in life. His eyes bore into mine, waiting for a response.

"Okay."

Chapter Twenty

I stared into my wife's eyes. It was weird to think that I was a married man now. All the hook-ups and fuck-ups from before are now over with. Nothing can really change over the course of a few moments, but in my mind, everything had changed. Being a husband meant taking care of my family, even if my family was only Raven...for now. Were kids something she would want? Most couples had that conversation way before they got married. We obviously didn't have that luxury, but we had our whole lives to figure each other out. If she wanted kids, I had no problem giving them to her. And if she didn't, I'd be fine with that too. A piece of her red hair fell from the updo, and I didn't hesitate before reaching out and tucking it behind her ear. Her chest stopped moving as if she was holding her breath.

"So what now?" she asked quietly.

I leaned back into the chair and took a drink. "Now we enjoy being married for a day, go back to the Bronx tomorrow, and, soon, we'll be the owners of the brothel. Problem solved."

A hint of a smile ghosted her lips, but it was gone again before I could engrave it into my memory.

"You're not going to try to take over the brothel once we own it, right?" she asked.

"Not unless you want me to. Although, I think it could use some updates to make it a little more upscale."

She bit her lips, but I could see the gears turning in her head. If we could update the brothel and keep a couple men stationed there, it would bring in better clients who would pay a lot more. Raven wouldn't feel bad about taking a bigger cut of money from each transaction if the men were paying twice as much as they're paying now. I might not know a lot about the brothel like Raven does, but I knew a shit-ton about running a business.

"Upgrading would be nice," she finally said.

I nodded. We both finished our drinks before making our way up to the bedroom to consummate our marriage.

*****

Our time in Italy seemed to fly by, and before I knew it, we were back in the Bronx. Raven was still getting over her jet lag. She was asleep when I snuck out of the house. I was happy for that, considering I didn't want to have to explain to her what I was going out to do.

It was hard to track her friend Ben down, the one that she'd bought the brothel from, but I finally found out where he was staying. Jacob, my private investigator, had to do some digging to find the location, which made me think that Ben knew at some point he'd be in danger for the stupid stunt he pulled.

I took a day trip out to Arizona to surprise him. When I pulled up to the two-story family home, I knew the Irish must have given him a good amount of money to keep his mouth shut. I wonder how much money it cost to screw over someone that considered you a friend. Respect was everything in Cosa Nostra, and men who didn't have it disgusted me. I knocked on the door as Cal stood behind me, looking intimidating as hell. The door opened and a woman stood with a baby on her hip. It caught me off guard, but my surprise was quickly replaced with anger. While Raven was terrified of her girls being taken away, this man had been playing house with the money he used to scam her.

I cleared my throat, trying to keep my temper at bay. "Is Ben here?"

The woman's eyes shifted to Cal briefly. "Give me just a moment."

She attempted to close the door, but I put my foot in between the door and the frame.

"We'd love to wait inside," I said with a sadistic smirk. Now, the woman looked scared, but she didn't say anything as we both walked into the house.

"Ben, you have a visitor!" she yelled up the stairs.

I could hear his footsteps on the stairs, but as he came around to the last flight and peeked around the corner, he took off, running back up the steps. Cal ran off after him, and I followed close behind. Ben was trying to open the window when Cal grabbed him around the waist and threw him to the floor. The man was a twig and probably weighed less than Cal benched.

"Take a seat," I said, tilting my head toward the bed in the middle of the room. The man got off the floor and lowered himself onto the mattress. He already looked like he was about to shit his pants. The baby downstairs started to cry.

"Make sure the wife doesn't call the cops," I told Cal. That was the last thing I needed.

Cal grunted and walked past me back down the steps.

"I did what you asked, I don't know what more you want. Please just leave," Ben begged.

I raised an eyebrow. "And what did we want?"

"For me to get rid of the brothel."

"Who told you to sell the brothel?"

Ben kept his mouth shut as he realized we weren't with the Irish.

I let out a sigh. "You have a beautiful family downstairs. If you want to keep this little perfect life you have, I suggest you start talking."

"What more do you want from me?"

"Who told you to get rid of the brothel!" I shouted, losing my patience.

"The Irish. I was told to sell it and disappear. They gave me a lot of money."

The gears started to turn.

"Did you have a loan for the brothel?" I asked.

Ben shook his head. "No, I never got involved in anything like that. I keep my distance from other businesses. I ran the brothel and I went home...until the Irish told me to sell it and disappear."

It finally made since. Ben didn't sell Raven a bad business. The Irish has been acting like she owes them so they can get money out of her. Then, when she runs out of money, they'll take the girls and sell them overseas. It was genius, really.

I smiled a malicious grin. "Well then, I guess today is your lucky day. I don't have to break your kneecaps."

*****

"Are you out of your fucking mind?!" Giovanni spat, barely holding on to his thin thread of control.

"You said she didn't have protection because we weren't married."

"No, I said she didn't have protection because she wasn't family."

I shrugged. "Same thing."

"So what's going to happen after this is all over, Enzo? We don't believe in divorce."

I wanted to call him a hypocrite, considering he had just recently divorced his wife, but I figured it was smarter to keep my mouth shut.

He ran a hand down his face before turning around in his chair and grabbing a bottle of scotch off the shelf. I watched as he poured himself a glass and drank it in one gulp. It was silent in the office since we were the only ones at his nightclub. The club wasn't open yet, but this was where Giovanni did most of his work. Anytime one of the capos needed to meet with him, we could almost guarantee he'd be here.

"I tracked down the asshole who sold the brothel to Raven. The Irish paid him to sell the brothel to someone else and disappear so that they could lie and say the brothel had a debt on it. There's never been a debt. They're trying to extort as much money as possible from her before they take the girls and sell them on the black market."

I've been thinking to come up with a solution. The only thing that made sense was to offer them money, but I wasn't even sure if they'd take it.

Giovanni let out a frustrated breath. "I'll set up a meeting with Connor. I'll let you know the time and place. We'll offer five hundred thousand, not a penny more."

I didn't think they were going to accept it. Sex trade was a multi-billion dollar industry. They could get more than five hundred thousand for one girl, but Giovanni was meeting me halfway, so I agreed.

"Now get the fuck out of my office," he said.

I got up from the chair and walked out before he could change his mind. The office opened up to a private lounge area, and I crossed the room before taking the back stairwell outside. My phone rang. Cal's name flashed across the screen. I picked up as I got into my car.

"Boss," Cal said.

"What's up?"

"Your girl is freaking out. She keeps throwing shit and wouldn't stop until I called you," he said, his voice holding an apology in it.

Fuck, she's crazy, but I love her for it.

"Put her on the phone."

Something rustled on the other end of the line before her voice came through.

"They took Erica!" Her voice broke as she spoke, as if on the edge of tears. My body went rigid as I thought about someone making my wife cry.

"Erica? From the brothel?" I asked.

"They took her—"

"Sit tight." Fuck, I wasn't fast enough. I hung up and quickly dialed Harris, who's supposed to be stationed outside the brothel. When it went to voicemail, I knew something was seriously wrong. I started the Lamborghini and headed straight to the brothel.

Everything looked quiet until I opened the front door, and then chaos erupted. The girls were in the lobby in various states of shock as they stared at the body in the middle of the floor. Harris had been shot in the head, and from the way his body fell, it looks like they made him get on his knees beforehand. The women must have witnessed everything. Some were crying hysterically while others looked completely paralyzed with fear.

"Fuck." Harris had worked for me for years, and he was a damn good solider too. I knew he wouldn't have gone down without a fight. Pain tugged at my chest.

"They took her...they took Erica," one of the girls stuttered through tears.

I turned away from them and called Cal back.

"Boss," he greeted.

"I need you to bring Raven over to the brothel and get the clean-up crew here."

*****

Raven was able to get the girls to calm down despite the frenzy she'd just been in moments before. Once everyone was upstairs, my crew came in, removed the body, and cleaned up the mess. I found Raven in the kitchen, leaning against the counter with a mug of hot coffee in her hand. Her eyes were puffy and her hair was down, but it wasn't silky or straight like I was used it. It looked like she'd been rolling around in my bed. I preferred her hair this way.

"How did you know she was missing?" I asked, taking a step closer to her.

She jumped as if just realizing I'd walked into the room.

"I don't want to get anyone in trouble," she said quietly.

I raised an eyebrow. "Why would someone get in trouble?"

"Because I'm your prisoner, right? I'm not supposed to have access to the outside world."

I shook my head. "All of that changed when you put that ring on your finger. If you want to go somewhere, just let Cal know."

"You took my phone," she said.

Shit, I'd forgotten about that. "I'll get you a new one," I assured her.

"Cal lets me use his phone sometimes to call and check on the brothel."

"I thought you didn't like him."

She shrugged. "I've warmed up to him."

We stood there in silence for a moment.

"What are they going to do to her?" she asked, wiping at her face. I gathered her in my arms and then she really started to cry. The tears shook her small body, and she was soaking my T-shirt. The smell of her shampoo filled my noise, and I ran a hand down her back as she sobbed. She'd been so strong when Cal pulled up with her at the brothel, but now it was all coming out. Everything she'd been holding in was finally breaking the surface.

"We'll find her."

"Promise me," she demanded, pulling back to look into my eyes. Her face was streaked with tears.

I hesitated. There was no telling where Erica could be or even if she was alive.

"Promise me you'll find her," she repeated. She had never asked me for anything in the entire time we've known each other.

"I promise."

Chapter Twenty-One

"What do you think you could do that my men can't?" Enzo asked. I wanted to stay at the house with the girls, but he was right. I was no stronger than the men outside guarding the place.

"If they come back, it might be you they take next time, and I'm not willing to have you in that situation. No fucking way."

I wanted to tell him that it wasn't his choice, but he'd done so much for me already that I kept my mouth shut. "Okay."

He raised an eyebrow in surprise. "You're not going to fight me on this?"

I shook my head. "You promised me you would get Erica back. I'm trusting you...don't let anything happen to the rest of them."

I hoped he understood the weight of my words. Trust was stronger than anything else I could give him. Stronger than love. It was something I hadn't given to anyone because when you trust someone, you risk getting stabbed in the back. I trusted my husband. It was a weird thought to have. He's taken care of me up to this point, even when I refused to acknowledge that I needed it. I took comfort in knowing that everything didn't fall on my shoulders. Sharing the burden was a relief I wasn't used to.

He nodded. "Let's go home."

I told the girls goodbye before getting in Enzo's Lamborghini. He drove in silence, both of us lost in our thoughts. Once we were in the apartment, Bello came running toward me. I bent down to pet behind his ears. I was never a big animal person, but I'd instantly taken to Bello. When Enzo was gone all day, Bello kept me company. I couldn't imagine staying in the apartment without him.

"You hungry?" Enzo asked.

"I could eat."

I stood up from petting Bello and took a seat on the stool. Enzo reached in the fridge and pulled out various ingredients. He made two omelets and put them on plates before joining me at the island to eat.

"We'll find her. The Irish have a few locations where they could be keeping her."

I nodded. "I know, Enzo."

I didn't want to think about it anymore. I can only imagine the type of shit that could be happening to Erica right now. I was trying hard to keep my mind from going to that place. We ate in silence, and once we finished, I took both plates to the sink. When I turned around, Enzo was standing in front of me. My chest brushed against his own as I breathed. His cologne filled my nose, mixed with the subtle hint of marijuana smoke.

"You smell like weed," I said.

"I was at Giovanni's club before I heard about the brothel."

He bent his head down and nipped the side of my neck. My body instantly responded to his touch. I needed him, right now, needed his comfort so I could take my mind off all the dark thoughts trying to reach the surface. I didn't want to think; I only wanted to feel. I let out a moan as his mouth moved down my neck to my chest, sucking against the side of my breast.

"Enzo..."

He grabbed me around the waist and, as if I weighed nothing, set me on top of the counter. He gave me some distance as I quickly undressed. He did the same until we were both completely naked. The coldness of the metal under my skin should have made me shiver, but I was so warm, I barely noticed. He stepped between my legs, and I wrapped my arms around his neck, pressing my breasts against his naked chest. I wanted to feel his body all over me. I wanted to feel the weight of him on top of me and to be surrounded by his scent. I needed that more than anything. He kissed me, at first gentle and hesitant, but I increased the pace, letting him know I wasn't going to break. I wasn't a china doll sitting on the ledge of a shelf. I was a bowling ball that crashed but never broke, but I still needed his support to stay steady because right now, I didn't want to fall. He reached between my thighs to feel the moisture that was dripping onto the counter.

"Fuck, baby," he said, breaking away from our kiss as he rubbed his finger in a circular motion around my clit. My body vibrated as he increased his speed. My muscles tensed as he brought me close to the edge. I was hyper-aware of my nipples rubbing against his muscular chest.

"Right there," I moaned. He pulled away, but before I could complain, he grabbed his dick and guided it between my folds. He moved up and down, making sure to stimulate my clit. I grabbed onto his arms, my nails digging into him deep enough to break skin.

"Enzo, I'm going to come."

"Look at me," he commanded. I hadn't even realized I'd closed my eyes, but they flutter open at his voice. I focused on his green eyes as I unraveled. My legs shook, and the air is sucked out of my lungs as the warm sensation starts at my toes and moves all the way up to the top of my head. I didn't had time to come down before Enzo grabbed my hips and lifted me up before impaling me on his cock. His hands grabbed my ass, and it took all my strength to keep myself wrapped around him so I didn't fall as he moved me up and down his length. My walls were so tight from the orgasm, his dick felt especially filling. My pussy rubbed against his body to the point that it was almost too much.

"Shit," I moaned.

"One more time," he demanded

"I can't." My body was weak.

"Yes, you can. One more time."

He bent down and bit my neck, sending me over the edge again, before he let out a groan and emptied himself inside me.

Chapter Twenty-Two

<u>Enzo</u>

My leg bounced as we drove to the bar. I was barely keeping my anger in check, and my adrenaline was running high. Giovanni's eyes flickered to me from the driver's seat.

"Don't say shit when we get in there. You already look like you're ready for a fight."

I took a deep breath, trying to get myself under control. Raven cried last night because of those assholes. It could have easily been her they'd taken. The thought of that possibility was enough to piss me off. Giovanni parked the all-black Mercedes out front before getting out. I followed behind him. It was the middle of the day, but the Irish bar was filled with smoke, and three people sat at the bar looking like they've been there for a while. Connor sat in a chair by himself, waiting for us. He waved at the two chairs across the table from him. He wore dark jeans and a black button-down shirt. His reddish-brown hair was pushed back away from his face, so his dark green eyes looked more prominent. He was the opposite of Niall, the previous boss of the Irish mob. While Niall had been fat with a slight drinking problem, Connor actually looked like he had his shit together.

"Take a seat," Connor said.

Usually, Gio made some smart-ass comment when someone told him what to do, but he was trying to get them on our side.

"What brings you to our side of town? I thought everything was clear. We'll stick to our business, you stick to yours," Connor asked.

"Everything is working out fine for us," Giovanni confirmed.

Connor raised an eyebrow. "Yeah?"

"We have a business proposition for you," Giovanni said, cutting to the chase.

Connor leaned forward and placed his elbows on the table. "I'm listening."

"Five hundred thousand dollars for the brothel on Moorside Path."

Connor shifted his jaw as if thinking it over. "I like that," he said, taking me by surprise. I thought this meeting was going to be pointless. "I'm getting bored of it anyways."

Giovanni smirked, proud of this easy victory. "One more thing."

Connor's lips twisted into a smile. "You ask for a lot, Giovanni. Did you ask my father for this many favors as well? I don't want to give you the impression that we're on friendly terms."

"I would never assume that. We need the girl back."

Connor tilted his head. "What girl?"

"The girl you took from the brothel last night after shooting my man," I said.

Giovanni glared at me.

"Enzo, right? I think you're mistaken. My men have stayed cleared of the brothel. In fact, I was hoping you'd offer me something for it in light of your recent marriage."

Giovanni and I shared a quick look. Connor glanced between us.

"Looks like you got another enemy on your hands. I'll take my money in cash tonight," Connor said. He stood up from the table. We stood as well. We shook hands with Connor before exiting.

"That can't be true," I blurted out as soon as we got in the car. "They have a warehouse off Fifth Street. That's probably where they're keeping her."

"No."

I turned to face Giovanni. "What do you mean 'no'?"

"We're not breaking into their warehouse. We solved the problem, and we're lucky that Connor took the deal and didn't fight us on this. I'm not causing more issues to save some girl. We're not superheroes, Enzo."

*****

"Did you find her?" Raven asked as soon as I walked in the door. She was dressed in one of my T-shirts and a pair of tight yoga pants. Her red hair fell past her shoulders. I rubbed a hand over my face, not wanting to tell her the bad news. I promised her I'd find her friend, and I wasn't in the position to break promises.

"The Irish claim they don't have her."

Her eyes widened. "That's not possible."

"I know." I walked past her to sit down on the couch. "They claimed they didn't break into the brothel last night or kill Harris. I know it sounds crazy, but I don't know why they would lie. They have no reason to lie to us."

Something wasn't adding up.

Raven stood with her arms crossed over her chest. I motioned to the other side of the couch. "Sit."

She uncrossed her arms and joined me on the couch. She let out a sigh and sank into the cushion. "Enzo, she could be anywhere by now."

"I know, but I promised you I'd find her." I just had to figure out where to look.

She was silent, probably lost in her own thoughts. I slung my arm over the back of the couch, and she leaned into me. Her hair smelled like vanilla. I rested my chin on top of her hair.

"Cosa Nostra bought the brothel from the Irish," I said.

She lifted her head. "Really?"

I nodded. "Five hundred thousand."

"So I can go back?" Her eyes filled with hope.

"Do you want to go back?" I asked. I liked her here in my apartment every time I came home. I liked knowing that she was safe and surrounded by my men. Now that we were married, she would always be a target, but she was also now under our protection.

She raised an eyebrow. "Why wouldn't I?"

"We're married. It's not like you need the money."

She tilted her head to the side. "I'm just supposed to leave the girls to fend for themselves?"

"I can get someone to take your place."

She scoffed. "You mean a man who probably won't give a shit about anything except money."

"It's a business, baby."

She pushed me away and stood to her feet. "Those girls are not there to generate money for your precious mafia," she spat.

"A lot of them are trying to get back on their feet. I could have easily been one of them, so don't sit here and tell me it's just a business."

I stared at her but didn't say anything. I understood how much she cared for these girls, but she had a life too and now a husband. Was this really all she wanted? To run a brothel for the rest of her life? As my wife, she could have anything she wanted. When she didn't get a reaction out of me, she stormed off. The door to our bedroom slammed shut. A few moments later, she came out dressed in a pair of tight jeans and a sweater.

"Where are you going?"

"To work."

I shook my head, resisting the urge to roll my eyes. "Stop with the dramatization."

She glared at me but didn't say anything before snatching a pair of keys off the entry table and leaving.

Chapter Twenty-Three

I didn't go straight to the brothel like I'd planned. Instead, I found myself at Toby's bar. Before I left the apartment, I grabbed a pair of keys, not having any idea what it went to. I was relieved to find they belonged to a nice Lexus and not one of the sports cars that I had no idea how to drive. Finding a parking spot on the street outside the bar was a struggle. I had to park three blocks away. I should be scared to be walking alone, but I knew Enzo probably had someone looking after me, and from what he said, the rock on my finger was protection in itself. The ring felt a lot heavier than it had before. Maybe because I finally realized what it meant to be married to a made man. And not just any made man. A capo. Enzo ruled the Bronx, and this ring meant I was his partner.

I opened the door to the bar and loud music poured out. The place almost looked more like a nightclub. What the hell? Then I noticed the handmade sign behind the bar.

Burgers $5

Hot Dog $3

Chip & Soda $1

Shit, I'd completely forgotten about the barbecue. I can't believe how much has changed since Toby had told me about it. I hadn't even gotten the chance to let the girls know. I didn't spot Toby, so I took a seat on the only open barstool.

"What can I get you?" The bartender asked me. She was petite with hair that went down to her waist.

"Is Toby here tonight?" I asked.

The girl looked uncomfortable. If I knew anything about my brother, there were probably a lot of crazy girls who came up here looking for him after he snuck out of their house after a one-night stand.

"I'm his sister," I clarified when the girl didn't respond.

"He's in the back. I'll grab him."

She walked away, and I took my time to look around the bar. After a moment, Toby came out of the back room and smiled at me.

"Hey! What's up?" he asked.

"Maybe I just wanted to see my brother and get some good barbecue."

He smiled and made me a martini. I took a sip. "Damn, that's good."

"I hope so. I've been bartending for long enough. I should know how to make a martini."

When I didn't respond, he tilted his head. "What's going on Raven?"

"Someone took Erica," I said quietly.

His eyes widened. "What?! Who?"

"We don't know. We thought it was the Irish, but Enzo doesn't think so."

"Enzo?" he lowered his voice to a whisper too. "You're involved with him?"

I forgot all the things I still haven't told Toby. Heat traveled up my neck. "Actually, we're married."

His eyes landed on my hand where the ring sat. It was impossible to miss.

"Holy shit...congratulation? When did this happen? And why?"

"It's a long story and you have a full bar to take care of," I said, not wanting to pull him away from his business.

"I have time." He came from around the bar and I followed behind him. He led me to the back exit where an old beaten down picnic table sat next to a dumpster. This must be where his employees came out to take their smoke breaks. We sat at the picnic table and I explained everything. The words rapidly fell from my lips, like I'd been waiting to tell someone, anyone, what was going on. It was nice to get everything off my chest, and Toby was the perfect sound board. He would have an outsider's perspective on all of this. He kept quiet throughout my whole story.

"Wow," he said after I was done. He ran his hands through his hair. "So Enzo, huh?"

I nodded my head and took a drink of the martini.

"Do you love him?" Toby asked.

I rolled my eyes. "He forced me to marry him."

"You didn't answer the question."

I looked down at the table. I had strong feelings for Enzo, I couldn't deny that. "How can I love someone that hasn't given me that chance to decide if I want to be with them?"

"Would you choose to be with him?"

I was silent.

He let out a sigh. "You have an opportunity here, Raven. You always wanted a family, and you just married into the most notorious and largest family in North America. Do you really want to work at the brothel for the rest of your life?"

"Yes," I said immediately. The brothel is where I found my place. I was good at my job, and I want to continue to build the business. I'm not ready to give up on it yet.

"Then you need to figure out how that's going to fit in with your new family. You're so used to doing everything on your own. I get it. I think Enzo is just giving you a chance to walk away, but if you don't want to walk away, then you need to tell him that. Tell him how important the business is to you—"

"He should already know how important it is to me." Enzo has witnessed the lengths I'd go to protect the brothel.

"Then remind him."

I swallowed the last of my martini in one big gulp. Toby smiled and stood from the table. He reached his hand out, and I grabbed it, using his hand to help me stand from the picnic table.

"Grab some barbecue before you go," he said before wrapping me up in a hug. It was rare for me to show affection, but I hugged him back.

"Thank you, Toby."

"Anytime, and who knows, I might need a favor from the king of the Bronx one day."

I laughed and playfully slapped his arm before we headed back inside.

Chapter Twenty-Four

Enzo

"Where's your wife?" Cole asked as I held the door open for him so he could walk into my apartment.

"I don't know," I replied, closing the door behind him.

Cole raised an eyebrow in question.

"She stormed off after I asked if she still wanted to work in the brothel," I clarified, even though I didn't need to. I walk past him down the hall to my office, and Cole followed behind me.

"Women," he mumbled.

I grabbed the bottle of scotch off the shelf behind my desk and poured him a drink. Usually, I'd have a drink too—God knew I needed one—but with Raven not at the apartment, if I had to jump into action, I needed to be sober.

"It doesn't make sense. All I did was ask a valid question. She doesn't *have* to work there anymore. I just wanted to make sure it's what she wanted."

Cole swirled his drink but didn't say anything.

"What?" I asked.

"You really want my opinion?" Cole asked.

I let out a sigh and sat down in the oversized chair. "Go ahead."

"She risked her life to get the money to save that place. Then, she agreed to marry a man she barely knew, and now, she's giving up all her control because she believes you can save her friend. She did all that for the brothel. Your question is insulting."

Fuck. Cole was right. She never asked for my help. I was the one who swooped in and felt the need to save her. It was like a punch in the gut, knowing that she really didn't need me. She was strong, and I should have known that she wasn't just going to just give up everything she'd worked for because I put a ring on her finger—a ring that I had assured her meant nothing except that I would protect her. I was trying to force a true marriage out of something that happened out of necessity.

My phone vibrated against the desk. My screen showed an unknown number. I looked up at Cole, but he just shrugged his shoulders. I snatched the phone and pressed it to my ear, waiting for the person on the other end to start talking.

"Hello? Raven?" The sound of the woman's voice made me sit up straight in my chair.

"Erica?" I asked. "This is Enzo. Where are you?"

There was rustling on the other side of the phone before a male voice came over the speaker.

"Wouldn't you like to know?"

What the fuck? I raked my brain, running through my enemies. Who would target the brothel? I pulled the phone away from my ear and put it on speaker so Cole could listen in.

"Who is this?" I asked, barely keeping my anger in check. Obviously, the man was stupid if he thought he was going to get away with this.

"You think you can kill our people without consequences? The mafia needs to stay the hell away from our neighborhoods like we've warned you. The Bronx isn't afraid of you."

My eyes meet Cole's across the desk. It had to be the street gang. I'd almost forgotten about them in the chaos of everything else going on.

"If you ever want to see your girl—"

The laugh that bubbles out of me cut off whatever the man was about to say. The idiot thought they had Raven.

"If you really think I'm going to negotiate with you, you have another thing coming."

Cole pulled a device out from his pocket and set it next to the phone. We would have their location in a matter of minutes. It was almost too easy.

"What's your plan after this? Kidnap my girl, get me out of your neighborhood, and then what? You think you'd live to see the next day? You're coming after the biggest criminal organization in North America with a half-assed plan and a twenty-person gang. You're a fool."

A red light on the device lit up, and Cole gave me the thumbs up. I rose from my chair and tucked my Desert Eagle into the back of my jeans.

"It's been nice talking to you, but I have somewhere to be."

I hung up before the man could respond. In the back of my head, I knew there was the possibility that they would kill Erica and run, but I had to hold out hope that the gang would stay still until I could reach them. I walked out of the apartment with Cole right on my heels.

"Call Tommy and give him the location. He'll want to be involved," I told Cole as we got into the elevator. I didn't need a lot of men; one of my guys could take out half of the gang by himself.

"Got it, Boss." Cole punched in Tommy's number and pressed the phone to his ear. I took out my phone and called Giovanni. He picked up on the second ring.

"What's up?"

"We found Erica. She's across town. That low-level street gang took her," I said.

Giovanni let out a whistle. "Damn, they have balls. How many men are you taking?"

"Four, including me. I'm calling in Tommy, and I got Cole."

Giovanni was quiet on the other line. "That should be good. Go by the warehouse to pick up some weapons."

"Got it. I'll call you when I'm done."

I slid into the Lamborghini with Cole when a thought popped into my head. I had one more person to call. Even though I wasn't worried about this street gang, I knew Raven would kill me if I walked into something like this without talking to her. Before Raven, I never would have thought about my own safety in a situation like this. I lived for the action that came with being a capo, but now I had someone else to worry about. I promised Raven I'd get Erica back, but I'd also made a promise to myself that I'd keep Raven safe. I needed to be alive in order for that to happen.

*****

"We're stopping by the warehouse. Grab whatever you need and an AK for the rest of us," I told Cole. He'd want to use a sniper rifle.

"You worried they'll try something crazy?" Cole asked.

I shook my head. "They're in over their heads."

I parked outside of the warehouse. Once Cole was inside, I called Raven.

"Hey," her voice came over the speakers of the car. The sound was like a melody, and it instantly relaxed me. My shoulders dropped. I half-expected her to still be mad after our earlier talk.

"I'm on my way to get Erica," I said.

"You found her! Where is she?!"

"Some people took her. I don't have time to go into detail. I just want you to know that I'm on my way to get her."

There was a moment of silence on the other line.

"Enzo...promise me you'll be okay," she said, her voice taking on a warning tone.

"You've been asking me to promise a lot," I tried to joke, but she didn't laugh. "I'm going to be fine. I'll take care of this and then we can talk when I get home. I'm sorry about...all of this."

Raven never really asked for my help, but I stepped in anyways, and I still wasn't sure if I made her life better or worse by doing that.

"I'm sorry too. We'll talk when you're home safe."

I didn't miss the way she referred to my apartment as home. I hung up just as Cole came out of the warehouse with a gigantic black duffel bag slung over his shoulder. Disguising that many guns was a challenge, but it's not like I was worried about the police. Cosa Nostra had most of the cops in our back pocket. Cole threw the guns in the back before getting in the passenger seat.

"You ready for this?" I asked him.

Cole nodded. "Always."

*****

The address was for a hotel in the middle of the fucking city, which meant too many fucking witnesses.

"They're fucking idiots. They took her and have been keeping her in a hotel room," I said, looking around the sidewalk at all the people. The sun had set, but it was still early in the evening, so people walked the streets. Maybe this is what they wanted. Maybe they think I won't go after them in the middle of the city. They're wrong. I couldn't give a fuck about all these people. The mob runs this city, and I made a promise to my wife. I looked in the rearview mirror to see Tommy pull up behind me. Cole got out of the car first and grabbed the big duffel bag.

"What's the plan?" Tommy asked, meeting me behind the Lamborghini. He had a man from his crew with him that I didn't recognize. I haven't had time to think of a plan, but I was good on my feet. I looked at the big duffel bag on Cole's shoulder.

"We're not going to need that." I might not care about witnesses, but I also wasn't going to be obvious. "Grab the silencers I have under my seat," I told Cole. "You packin'?" I asked Tommy.

Tommy raised his eyebrow. "You serious?"

It was a stupid question. Of course he was packin'. Cole opened the car door and set the duffel bag back inside.

"No plan. We find out what room they're in, and we take care of them. This is going to be easier than I thought."

Cole handed out the silencers, and we screwed them onto our handguns.

Tommy nodded. "Let's go."

I led the way into the hotel. A couple people were in the lobby sitting on a couch. The receptionist, a young man dressed in the company's dark green uniform, stood at the front desk. His name tag read Jerry. The hotel wasn't upscale by any means, so we looked slightly out of place. Not that it mattered. The man's eyes widened as we got closer to the desk.

"I need to know what room they're in," I told the man.

He blinked twice as if not hearing me correctly. "Um...who...whose room?" he stuttered.

I grabbed the gun from my back and casually set it on the desk. "I don't have much time, Jerry. You know exactly who I'm looking for, because when they checked in this hotel, you feared this exact situation. They were also probably dragging a woman along with them who didn't look too willing."

I could almost hear the man's heart racing. His hand shook as he reached behind the desk and grabbed a key card. He slid it across the desk to me.

"Room 501."

I flashed him a smile. "Thank you."

I walked away with the key card in my hand. We all huddled in the elevator.

"I'll take out the hallway cameras on the floor," Cole said.

I nodded. I hadn't even thought about that. The elevator doors opened to a hallway with old green carpeting. Cole went ahead of us, breaking the cameras off the walls. I looked behind me to see Tommy and a man from his crew with their handguns out. I clenched my hand around my Desert Eagle as room 501 came into view. Cole looked at me and nodded, signaling that all the cameras were gone. I could hear the sound of voices on the other side of the door. I took a deep breath before kicking the door in. Five men all jumped up from their seated position. I didn't hesitate before opening fire on one of the guys to the left of the door. The other men scurried, probably trying to find where they put their gun. Amateurs.

"If you point a gun at me, I'll kill you. Your chances of coming out here alive are up to you," I said between gritted teeth.

Two of the men stopped searching. Cole and Tommy stepped into the room. Tommy used the butt of his gun to hit one of the men over the top of the head. The man passed out, his body slumping to the floor. The only man left raised his gun and aimed, but I was faster. I pulled the trigger, and the man's body jerked from the impact.

"Ah, fuck!" the man screamed out. The cops would be here any minute. I was sure the receptionist had called by now. As if Tommy could read my mind, he pulled out his phone and called Giovanni.

"We need footage from the Double Tree hotel deleted. The cops will be here soon and we're still here." He paused listening to Giovanni's response. "Yes, Boss," he said before hanging up.

"Gio's on it, but we need to get the fuck out of here."

I scanned the room, looking at what we were dealing with. One man was passed out on the floor. One was dead. Two more stood frozen with fear. Cole had his gun pointed at them so they wouldn't try to run. I looked at the last man on the floor, who had blood pooling from his arm. I tucked my gun into my waistband and crouched down next to the bleeding man.

"Where is she?" I asked.

"I don't—"

I grabbed his arm and twisted it. More blood squirted out onto the carpet.

"Ahhh!" he screamed.

"Now, I don't have much time, so I suggest you start talking."

"In the bathroom! Please! Fuck, man!"

I let go of the man, and he moaned as he rolled around the floor in agony. Tommy, Cole, and the guy from Tommy's crew watched as I crossed the room. I listened at the bathroom door for any sound. When I didn't hear anything, I opened the door to see a gun pointed at my face. I didn't have time to react before a shot rang out.

Chapter Twenty- Five

I drummed my fingers on the counter of the kitchen island as I waited for Enzo. My stomach was in knots. I hated that all I could do was sit here and cross my fingers. I wanted to help, but I knew Enzo wouldn't allow me to get involved. Erica must be terrified. The apartment door burst open and I jumped out of my chair. Cole and another guy were carrying Enzo. My stomach dropped as I saw the blood covering Cole's shirt.

"Enzo! Cole, what happened?!"

They rushed past me and laid Enzo down on the kitchen island. His eyes were open, and his face twisted in pain. I wanted to grab onto him, but there was blood everywhere. I couldn't tell where he was bleeding from.

"What the fuck happened?" I snapped, anger mixing with my fear.

"Doc is coming up here now. He got shot in the side," Cole said. I looked down at Enzo, noticing what looks like a sheet wrapped around his torso.

"It's not as bad as it looks," Enzo croaked, his voice filled with pain.

"It's not bad? You promised you'd be safe and you're bleeding on the table!" I retorted. I shouldn't be so angry at him, but I can't help it. The apartment door opens again, and a gray-haired man walked inside with a medical bag in his hand.

"He got shot on the left side, Doc," Tommy told the man. I moved to get out of the doctor's way as he looked over Enzo. I came to the other side of the island and grabbed Enzo's hand.

His green eyes looked up at me, and he reached a hand up to wipe at my face. I didn't even notice I'd started to cry. His face twisted in pain again as the doctor moved him.

"I got to cut this sheet off. You guys might want to leave. It could get pretty bloody."

Tommy and Cole left the room, but I stayed put. There was no way I was going to leave his side. The doctor gave Enzo some pain medicine and got to work removing the bullet and stitching everything up. By the time he finished, there was blood all over the kitchen, but at least it looked like Enzo wasn't in pain anymore. We hadn't said anything to each other while the doctor worked on him. I ran my thumb across our conjoined hands. Everything we needed to say to each other was in our shared gaze. We might disagree on things, but I couldn't lose him. Despite the twisted way we came together—the lies, deception, and forced marriage—the only person I wanted was Enzo. The doctor packed up his bag, and then gave me very strict instructions to make sure Enzo stays in bed and takes his medicine so he doesn't get an infection. Tommy handed the doctor a stack of rolled up cash and patted him on the back before he left.

"Let's get you into the bed while you're still rolling high on the morphine," I said.

Enzo smiled a sloppy grin. "I just got shot and you're already trying to get me in bed."

I couldn't help the smile that tugged at my lips.

I turned to Tommy. "Help me get him in the bedroom?"

Tommy came over and, together, we walked Enzo to our bedroom. I helped him change into clothes that weren't completely soaked in blood. All the while, he insisted that I was trying to fuck him because I found gunshot wound victims hot. It took everything I had not to laugh at this goofy side of Enzo, but doing so would only encourage him. Once he was asleep and tucked into bed, I slipped out of the room. Tommy and Cole were sitting in chairs across from each other, both focused on the phones in their hands.

Tommy lifted his eyes to look at me. "Cal is bringing Erica in," he said.

In the midst of seeing Enzo almost bleed out on the kitchen island, I'd forgotten about the reason he'd put himself in danger in the first place.

"She's here? Why—?"

"She was passed out when we found her. They must have drugged her. Cal has been watching over her in the car. She just woke up."

Fuck. What if the drugs they gave her triggered her addiction? The front door opened, and Erica's eyes were wide with a mix of confusion and fear as she slowly walked into the room. Cal stood behind her but didn't move.

"Erica!" I said before crossing the room and pulling her in for a hug. Tears streamed down my face, and Erica returned my hug. I'd been terrified since the moment Erica went missing. I pulled back to look over her. She looked fine, but that didn't mean anything. I placed my hands on both sides of Erica's face.

"Are you okay?" I asked.

Erica wiped at a tear that slid down her face. "Yeah, I'm okay. I don't remember much...I'm just really hungry."

I smiled, but then looked over at the kitchen. Blood was still caked on all the surfaces.

"I'll order you some take-out."

*****

Erica ate and showered before going to sleep in the guest bedroom. I didn't miss the way Cal hovered around her as if he still needed to watch over her. Tommy and Cole left after they had someone clean up the blood. The guy who'd shown up to clean the mess was young. He was probably trying to prove his worth to the mob, but I'd still felt bad as he scrubbed the kitchen clean of any traces of blood.

After what felt like the longest day in my life, I finally showered and changed into pajamas before laying in the bed next to Enzo. He laid on his back and raised his arms up as I got into bed, indicating he wanted my head on his chest. I curled into his good side and rested my head against his naked chest. I stared into the dark bedroom for a while, just feeling his chest rise and fall with each breath. His hand absentmindedly stroked my hair.

"Thank you...for everything," I said quietly.

"I promised you I'd get her back."

"You also promise me you'd be safe."

"I'm alive," he said.

I let out a breath of air. "Thank God. You scared the shit out of me."

"I know. I'm sorry."

A moment of silence passed between us. His breaths evened out as he fell asleep. A few minutes later, my eyelids became heavy and I drifted off.

*****

The smell of bacon made me snap my eyes open. I lifted my head up, expecting Enzo to be next to me, but the bed was empty. What the hell? I stood up and stumbled to the kitchen, where Enzo was leaning against the counter talking to Erica as she cooked.

"What the hell are you doing?" I barked at him. He narrowed his eyes at me as a silent warning. "You got shot less than twenty-four hours ago. Why are you up?"

"Babe, I can't lay in that bed all damn day."

I crossed my arms over my chest. "Then lay on the couch. I don't care where you lay, but you're going to rip your stitches."

His eyes roamed over my body, and his lips moved to one side as if debating if he should argue with me, but then he walked around me to lay down on the couch. I knew it would be a challenge to make Enzo sit still, but I didn't think it would be an issue so soon. I walked over to Erica as she brewed a fresh pot of coffee.

"How are you feeling today?" I asked her.

She shrugged. "I'm okay. Sleeping was hard. Since they kept me drugged the entire time, I think my body is confused, but Cal kept me company."

I looked down at her arm. There were fresh track marks where they must have stuck her.

"You don't have to make breakfast," I told her.

"Might as well. I couldn't sleep so I'm a little hyped up anyways."

I nodded and poured myself a cup of coffee. I added in creamer and sugar before making a cup for Erica.

"So who's running the house?" Erica asked.

I smiled. "Actually, I don't really know."

Erica laughed. "I'll go after breakfast."

I leaned against the counter and took a sip of my drink. "You really don't have to. You can stay here as long as you want, take some time to relax."

Erica gave me a sad smile. "Thanks, but it's probably better if I stay busy, go to a couple meetings. Try to focus on things that can distract me from..."

Her craving. She didn't need to say it out loud. I nodded and decided not to push her to rest and relax like I did with Enzo. Erica had dug herself out of a drug addiction before, so she must know how to do it again.

After we ate breakfast, Cal drove Erica back to the house. I took a seat on the chair next to the couch, but Enzo shook his head and sat up, making room for me.

I rolled my eyes but didn't argue as I got up to sit next to him. I leaned my head on his shoulder, feeling fatigue run through my body. I hadn't really done anything today, but I felt like I was at the end of a marathon. The stress that's been running through my body was finally over, and now, all that's left is exhaustion.

"So it's over now?" I asked Enzo.

He kissed the top of my head. "It's all over, baby."

"About the brothel..."

He let out a sigh as if he was dreading this talk just as much as I was. "Before all this happened, I talked to Cole. I didn't understand why you would want to keep working there when you didn't have to anymore. I had enough money to take care of us forever, and even if we got divorced, which isn't an option, you'd get half of everything."

I opened my mouth, but he pressed a finger to my lips.

"Let me finish. You shouldn't have to give up your entire life because I decided to step in and play Superman. It's not fair to you. I put myself in dangerous situations everyday, so I can't keep you from running the brothel if that's what you really want to do. I would never keep you from that. All I ask is that you let me increase security and invest in the business. I need to feel like you're safe because the clients are too scared to try anything stupid."

His green eyes stared into mine, waiting for a response. I wasn't sure what to say. I was ready to give up everything for Enzo, but he surprised me. Did I want to run the brothel? I thought about my life without it. My identity was more than just the owner of the brothel, but I enjoyed being around my girls. I wanted something to do during the day. I'd go mad sitting around Enzo's apartment all the time.

"I want to run the business. I like being there, and you're gone so much, I need something to entertain me. But I want you more. You're the one who makes me happy."

He nodded. "Then we just have to make sure you run it like a queen."

"Me and you, taking over the Bronx."

He smiled and kissed my forehead. "Baby, we already own the Bronx."

Epilogue

<u>Raven</u>

My heels clicked against the marble floors as I walked behind the desk.

"Go take care of your other businesses and stop hovering," I said to Enzo, who was leaned back in the desk chair, typing into his phone. Ever since we found out I was pregnant, he's been glued to my side. I was too early to even show, but Enzo acted like I was about to go into labor any second.

He looked up at me, his green eyes holding a playfulness in them. "They're our businesses and I'm taking care of them right from here."

Cal opened the door to the brothel, and a man in a suit walked in. I smiled at the John and got him checked in on the computer system before he took a seat in the waiting room. We'd renovated the entire house so it looked more like an office. The wooden floors on the main floor have been replaced with marble, and the old waiting couch has been replaced with an entire waiting room, complete with a TV that was always playing ESPN. The bedrooms were still upstairs, but there were only five instead of ten. Walls had been torn down to make the rooms bigger. The basement has been completely finished, including five newly built rooms. As promised Enzo doubled down on security, and the Johns would have to be stupid to try something. We also raised our prices significantly, which meant better clientele. The girls were making more money, so they didn't stick around for long. It made me happy that this place still served as a way for girls to do something temporary to get back on their feet.

"You can't sit around here my entire pregnancy," I told Enzo, placing a hand on my hip.

He rolled the chair closer before grabbing me around the waist and sitting me on his lap. I giggled in surprise.

He kissed my neck. "I. Can. Do. Whatever. I. Want," he said in between kisses.

I never thought I'd see the day when Enzo could sit still. Little did I know, all I had to do was get pregnant.

"Get a room," Erica said as she came down the steps. While most of the girls had left, Erica had stuck around. She was still managing her addiction by going to meetings twice a day. I flipped her the bird, and Erica laughed before going into the waiting room to grab her next client. I ground against Enzo's lap, and a low noise sounded in his chest.

"Don't provoke a lion," Enzo warned, his voice low and husky. A heat started in my belly, and Enzo placed a hand there as if he could sense it. I still couldn't believe I was going to have a baby. The life I lived now was so different than anything I ever imagined. Before Enzo, all I wanted to do was survive. I never imagined I'd be married with a baby. Our life was far from traditional. I was a madam for crying out loud, and Enzo dabbled in a little bit of everything. Our child wouldn't live a normal life. That was something I'd come to accept. But this was my family. After bouncing from foster home to foster home as a kid, I'd never imagined having a huge family. Toby was right. Cosa Nostra was my family.

Enzo's phone rang, interrupting our moment. He sighed and pulled it out. I got up from his lap.

"Enzo," he answered. He listened to the person on the other side of the phone. "I'll be there," he said before hanging up.

"Thank God," I joked. He stood and wrapped his arms around my waist.

"The Bronx needs you, Superman."

He nuzzled my neck. "The Bronx can fucking wait."

The End

What's next? Sign up for my newsletter to stay up to date on all new releases.

Notes

I hope you enjoyed reading *King of The Bronx*. Please consider leaving a review of this book. Reviews mean the world to indie authors.

ALSO BY K.D CLARK

The New York Capos Series:

Cassandra doesn't need a Prince Charming.

She has saved herself more times than she can count.

Life as the Boss of the biggest criminal organization in North America is not an easy job but maybe for one night she can forget about all that.

When she runs into a handsome man in her nightclub she doesn't ask any questions because she couldn't care less.

Cassandra is a boss but so is Andre and he's about to show her that he can be just as ruthless as her.

Standalones:

Savage Spades

The last thing Cam needs right now is the town's motorcycle club taking over her bar.

The failing bar that her father left her to deal with along with a loan from a dangerous man named Venom.

On top of that, she's trying to get through her classes without failing.

She doesn't have time for the blue-eyed monster of a man that can't keep his eyes off her.

But damn he would be a good distraction.

Dirty Empire

I married a monster.

Years ago my husband was the perfect man, until I was faced with his abusive side. I thought my husband would kill me but Maverick saved me. He seemed like my knight in shining armor. However, Maverick comes with his own set of baggage.

How will this tangled web of destruction and lust unravel? Dirty Empire will thrill, anger, push, and prod you to the edges of your imagination!

King of The Bronx

He belongs to the most notorious criminal organization in North America.

I watched him kill a man without blinking.

I've let him into my heart, and now I'm about to be his next target.

I need thirty-thousand dollars to save the only family I have, and the only way I know how to get it is by stealing from Enzo Genovese.

About the Author

K. D. Clark is a United States author living in Saint Louis, Missouri, with her high school sweetheart and being a dog mom to two amazing pit bulls. She spends every minute she can either working on her books or reading the great works of other romance authors. For more information on book releases and her writing process, please feel free to check out her website, Instagram, Facebook, and Twitter.

www.ingramcontent.com/pod-product-compliance
Lightning Source LLC
Chambersburg PA
CBHW030307160726
47992CB00005B/1916